There she wa

movie star in th

gorgeous doll that wet dreams are made of, standing on my doorstep with the hot Los Angeles sun lighting up her golden tresses. Warm as it was, she was wearing white mink over a gold lamé jumpsuit that was so tight it made her eyes bulge out almost as far as mine were. I opened the screen door and gestured for her to come in.

"Hello, Mac," she said breathily, lifting the mink stole off her shoulders. "Take my wrap, will you?"

"Forget it, baby," I snickered. "I'm not taking the rap for you or anyone else."

"Suit yourself," she said, pulling a small revolver out of a hidden pocket in the mink and pointing it at my chest. "I guess I'm just going to have to . . . kill you."

"Over my dead body," I said.

She smiled that sexy smile of hers and I saw her finger tighten around the trigger.

Also by the author:
The Case of the Hardboiled Dicks
The Official Hollywood Handbook
Love's Reckless Rash (co-written
under the pen name Rosemary Cartwheel)

Future Mac Slade Murder Mysteries:
Dial M for Room Service
Death Can Be Fatal
Tough Guys Don't Read Norman Mailer
Murder Most Fowl
Magnum Farce

the TINSELTOWN *Murders*

A MAC SLADE MYSTERY

John Blumenthal

A FIRESIDE BOOK
PUBLISHED BY SIMON & SCHUSTER, INC.
NEW YORK

A Fireside Book
Published by Simon & Schuster, Inc.
Simon & Schuster Building
Rockefeller Center
1230 Avenue of the Americas
New York, New York 10020

Designed by Levavi & Levavi
Manufactured in the
United States of America

10 9 8 7 6 5 4 3 2 1

Library of Congress
Cataloging in Publication Data
Blumenthal, John.
The Tinseltown murders.

"A Fireside book."
I. Title. II. Title: Tinsel town murders.
PS3552.L8485T5 1985 813'.54 85-2340
ISBN: 0-671-55539-1

The cheaper the cook, the gaudier the pâté.

—Jack Mushnik

The Mob goons were after me. Two Neanderthal behemoths with the combined IQ of a ficus tree, both with bushy eyebrows and sloping foreheads, both so big they made Moby Dick look like a box of fish sticks, both definitely on my case. They'd been trailing me for days now, making sure I didn't leave town until I paid up the lousy two G's I owed their boss, a Greek bookie named Cheap Louis Papadoupolis.

Ordinarily, I wouldn't have had this problem, but it was winter in New York City—the worst in five years—and I hadn't had a decent case come my way in months. The murder rate was down to practically nil, kidnapping was at a virtual standstill and even the thieves had all packed up and gone to Aruba instead of braving the elements and robbing people like they were supposed to. Hell, even the coppers were staying indoors. It was a pretty lousy state of affairs—a virtual outbreak of lawfulness—and I knew if things didn't thaw out soon, my dick business would be in the dumper financially. I was already down to my last bottle of rye, my last carton of butts, and my last twenty-five bucks. On the liability side, I was two months late on my office rent, my landlord had evicted me from my apartment, and I owed my ex three hundred simoleons in back alimony, not to mention the two thou I owed Louis. I knew it'd be a matter of days before the goons started showing up to play baseball with my kneecaps. I still had my Mastercard, but I needed dough, lots of it, and I needed it pronto.

The night before, my last resort had fallen through. Her name was Denise and I'd been dating her on and off for about two months. She was a good kid, a big blond number, about five eight in heels, six one barefoot, with a slim waist and a set of charlies that made it into the next room about twenty seconds before the rest of her got there. She wasn't the brightest dame I'd ever met but she owned her own manicure business and I figured she'd be good for a little dough.

We'd been out drinking and, as usual, she invited me back to her place for a nightcap. I poured us a couple of brandies while she changed into something comfortable—the usual black negligee—and the next thing I knew we were frolicking away like a bunch of sex-starved teenagers in the middle of her king-size waterbed.

When it was all over, I took a shower, put on my street clothes, and had her walk me to the door. We kissed good night for about ten minutes and I let her tongue explore the cracks in my bridge work for awhile before I pulled away from her.

"Listen, baby," I said, "you know I'm crazy about you, don't ya?"

"I could tell," she said, putting her well-manicured hands on my neck and whimpering something filthy in my ear.

"Ordinarily," I went on, "I wouldn't ask ya, but I need a favor real bad."

"Anything," she said, pouting. "Anything at all, Mac."

"See, the thing is," I explained, "things

have been a little tight for me lately. Business ain't so hot and I got debts out the whazoo."

"Poor Mac," she said sympathetically.

"So," I said, "I was wondering if you could see your way to giving me a little scratch."

"Sure, honeybuns," she said, and without another word, she lifted her hand to my cheek, dug her long fingernails into my flesh, and gave me a scratch that drew a line of blood down the side of my kisser. The next thing I knew, the door slammed in my face.

Of all the dumb moves, yours truly has to ask a professional manicurist for a little scratch. Next time a dame wanted to get wise with me, I'd pick one who bit her nails.

Anyhow, like I said, I was desperate for cash with no prospects in sight. I was digging around under my office carpet for loose pennies one blizzardy afternoon, when all of a sudden, there's a knock on the door. I could see the silhouettes of Cheap Louis' gargantuan mugs stopping most of the light from coming through the opaque window of my door, so before replying to the knock, I slid my roscoe into an open drawer to my left, just in case they decided to get nasty.

Just as I was absently wondering whether six slugs from a .38 would be enough to stop two charging Rhinos, the Rhinos in question barged into my office. Rhino Number One wore a plaid jacket with striped trousers and a madras tie, a nice combination if you happened to be a trained chimpanzee; Rhino Number Two wore black shirt, black trousers, black jacket, white tie—the standard Mob fashion statement. We stood there glaring at each other for about twenty seconds, before Rhino Number One finally got enough control of his motor reflexes to recall how to move his lips.

"You got da dough, Slade?" he said in a thick Brooklyn accent. "Cheap Louis wants his dough."

"I'm working on it," I said, letting my hand glide a little closer to my gat.

"Louis don't like welchehs," he said.

"Neither do I," I said. "Their grape juice is too sweet. So's their marmalade. But I hear Mott's makes a nice line of fruit drinks now. Tell Louis to try Mott's."

This stopped him for a second. He furrowed his half inch of brow and thought deeply for about half a minute. Meantime, his cretinous sidekick bashed his fist into the open palm of his other hand.

Finally, Rhino Number One, the one with the verbal skills, shrugged and nodded at his pal. "You want I should tell Butch here ta punch your lights out, Slade?"

I could tell Butch was just dying for a little rough stuff, so I let my hand slip closer to my gat.

"Tell him whatever you want," I said casually. "It's a free country."

"Punch his lights out, Butch," the goon said.

Butch smiled menacingly, tightened up his fist, and socked the living crap out of my desk lamp. It crashed against the wall, busting into smithereens. Next, he went over to my floor lamp and decked it with a hard left jab. The only remaining light was my overhead, but tall as he was, he couldn't reach it from the floor.

"Okay, okay, I've had enough," I said, as Butch started moving a footstool toward the ceiling light. "I told you I'm working on it, didn't I? The bank ought to be calling any minute now with my loan approval. Give me twelve hours."

"Cheap Louis wants his dough now," the first Rhino said. "Hand it over."

I glowered at him for about half a second and put my hand on the gat in the drawer. I was about to pick it up when all of a sudden I was saved by the phone. The ring startled me since I'd thought all along that the phone company had disconnected it.

"Must be the bank," I said, picking up the receiver but not taking my other hand off the roscoe.

"Hello?" I said pleasantly.

"Mac," a female voice said, somewhat frantically, "it's Gladys. Gladys Mushnik. Jack Mushnik's wife. I hope I'm not bothering you, but this is an emergency! Jack's in trouble and—"

"Yes, Mr. Chase," I said, in a singsong voice, strictly for the benefit of the two goons. "Yes, of course I can come right down to the *bank* to pick up the *money*." I smiled at the two rhinos, who were clearly disappointed at losing the opportunity to make cole slaw out of my face.

"Is that you, Mac?" Gladys asked, somewhat perplexed at my response. "Who's Mr. Chase? What bank? Jack's in trouble, Mac. He needs a friend—and since you and he were old army buddies I thought maybe you could come out to Los Angeles and straighten him out. I'm desperate, Mac! Jack won't listen to anyone but you. Will you come? Please?"

"Of course I'll come," I said. "Right away. Bye."

I hung up and straightened my tie. "Well, fellas, it's all straightened out," I said to the goons. "That was Mr. Chase himself."

The talkative Rhino was skeptical. "Who's dis Chase guy?" he asked.

"Haven't you two mugs ever heard of the Chase Manhattan Bank?" I asked. "What are you guys, cretins?"

"No, we ain't Cretans," the Rhino said. "Cheap Louis, he's a Cretan. Butch and me, we're Napolitanos."

"Fascinating," I said and motioned for the two thugs to follow me into the hallway as if we were on our way to my friendly neighborhood branch of the Chase Manhattan Bank. Like the dopes they were, they went right along with it. We stopped at the elevator and I pressed the down button.

The elevator doors swooshed open immediately and like a proper little gentleman, I gestured for the Rhino duet to enter before me. As soon as they were inside, and while their backs were still turned toward me, I reached in, pressed the second floor button and watched from the hallway as the elevator doors slammed shut, separating me from the goons. Then, as casual as can be, I strode for the stairs and walked down the twelve flights to the ground floor. On the third floor, I peered around the corner into the hallway and saw exactly what I knew I would see—the elevator needle was stuck between the second and third floors. Though it had been a royal pain in the butt since it had stopped working properly sometime around the Coolidge administration, and although I myself had been stuck once or twice in the damned thing, I knew that busted elevator would come in handy someday. Unfortunately for my goon friends, getting the thing to move once it was stuck between two and three required the services of an elevator technician.

It was snowing cats and dogs by the time I got outside, but lucky for me my heap started by the third turn of the key and I was off. Glancing down at the fuel gauge, I breathed a heavy sigh of relief—I had just enough gas left to make it to La Guardia.

❑

Ordinarily, I'm not this impulsive when it comes to transcontinental air travel, but number one, leaving town was preferable to kneecap surgery; number two, I figured the blizzard situation wasn't going to let up anytime soon and the old kisser could stand a little sunshine; and number three, Jack Mushnik was my best pal. He and I went back years and years. There isn't anything I wouldn't have done for old Jack. We'd been in the same dogface unit during the War—ten of the toughest, meanest dogfaces you'd ever want to meet—there was me, Jack, Blackie, Jip, Fido, Rover, Spot, a bunch of great guys if ever there was one. Jack had been my sarge and he'd looked out for me, been like a father to me. I'd been the rookie in the unit, and since I was only eighteen years old at the time, I'd been more than a little wet behind the ears. I'll never forget my first day on the front lines:

Bullets were whizzing around us and mortar shells were going off at regular intervals. We were crouched in a trench—all ten of us—waiting for the order to advance. I was sitting alone, scared out of my ever-loving wits, so scared that I was eating my K rations without first taking them out of their cellophane wrappers. Jack must have seen my hands shaking because he crouched beside me and took off his helmet.

"Whatsamatter, son?" he asked in a soft fatherly voice.

"Nothing, Sarge," I said bravely.

"You can tell me, son," he said. He looked me straight in the eye and I knew I could trust him.

"I'm scared, Sarge," I admitted in a tremulous voice. "I'm so damn scared I . . . I peed in my pants."

Jack put his hand on my shoulder and gave me that paternal look of his again. "That's okay, son," he said quietly. "It's okay to be scared."

"I just don't know if I can kill a man," I said. "I never killed anyone before."

"You'll be fine, son," he said.

"You think the other guys are scared too, Sarge?" I asked.

Jack looked around at the other dogfaces crouched near us. "Nope," he said. "None of them are, kid. You're the only lily-livered chickenshit in the group." Then he got up and put his helmet back on. "Hey, fellas," he said. "D'ja hear that? Private Slade here made a wee-wee in his skivvies."

I turned gratefully to him. "Thanks, Sarge," I said. "I needed that."

That was old Jack to the core—tough and gritty on the outside, tender and compassionate on the inside. A hell of a pal no matter what. And a hero, too. In fact, after the War, Jack got the Distinguished Service Cross for having flown eighty-five missions over Sicily, the most combat missions flown by anyone during the Korean War. On Armistice Day, we were both shipped to Los Angeles with the other guys from our unit. While I moved back to Manhattan, Jack stayed in Tinseltown, got a detective degree from the Ace Correspondence School of Detection, and started his own dick business with a GI loan. He did pretty well, and a few years later, he got himself a partner, a dick by the name of J.C. Quinn. Over the years, we'd kept in touch pretty regularly, but I hadn't heard from him since Christmas of 1982.

Except for a smattering of businessmen hiding behind copies of *The Wall Street Journal,* the plane was almost empty, so I had plenty of time to reminisce about good old Jack, and to try to figure out what exactly had gotten Gladys so worked up. Jack was no flake, that much I knew for sure—he was the straightest guy I'd ever met, a good husband, an honest dick, a guy you could trust. She had said she was desperate though—that much I remembered—so whatever it was that was troubling Jack, I knew it had to be serious.

The flight time passed quickly enough and only two out of the four working stewardesses tried to give me their phone numbers, but I managed to fend them off and catch a little shut-eye. The cranking noise of the landing wheels woke me up from a deep slumber, and before I knew it we were taxiing to the landing gate. Since I hadn't brought along any luggage except for what I had in my pockets, I was out of the airport and into a rental heap in a few minutes.

Jack and Gladys lived in a small two-bedroom bungalow in a second-rate area of the Valley. I took the freeway part of the way and then turned onto the surface streets. It was hotter than hell, but it felt nice compared to the weather I'd been in just a few hours ago. I opened the car windows and let the balmy Los Angeles breeze dry the sweat off my kisser.

❑

The front door was ajar so I let myself in. Gladys was in the kitchen starching a pair of Jack's undershorts when I rapped lightly on the formica counter to let her know I was there. She spun around on her heels and a look of surprise came over her face. Even in an old terry-cloth housecoat, she looked good. She'd been a B-movie star back in the early fifties but when she married Jack she gave up the screen for starching undershorts.

Without a word, she came over to me and gave me a nice friendly hug. Unfortunately, in her excitement she'd forgotten to put the iron down and suddenly I felt a triangular surge of heat burning an iron-size hole in the back of my one and only decent sports jacket.

"Oh, I'm so sorry, Mac!" she said sniffling. "I'm such a goose, sometimes."

"Never mind that," I said, slapping at my back. I put the iron down for her and gave her a good once-over. "You're a sight for sore eyes, Gladys," I said.

"I'm sorry," she said. "There's some Visine in the medicine cabinet."

"I mean you look great!" I said. But on closer examination, she didn't really look so hot. Her eyes were red from crying and it didn't look like she'd gotten much sleep lately, most likely on account of Jack.

"Now what's all this nonsense about

Jack?" I asked. "Where is the old war-horse anyway?"

At that she started to weep, burying her head in my shoulder. It was just a shower, though, because she pulled herself together in seconds and blew her nose on my lapel. I led her into the living room and we both sat down on the sofa.

"I haven't seen him or heard from him in three weeks," she said, sniffling. "He's . . . he's gone Hollywood or something."

"What exactly does that mean?" I asked.

"It means he's cashed in our savings and bought a Mercedes, wears chains around his neck, Gucci loafers on his feet, and hangs around expensive restaurants bragging about movie deals that don't exist. He even talks about movie stars he doesn't know from Adam as if they were his best friends."

"Jack?" I exclaimed, horrified and in disbelief. None of this sounded even remotely like the Jack Mushnik I knew.

"Not only that," she sniffed, "he's been hanging around with a pretty . . . gay crowd."

"Well, old Jack always liked to party—"

"No, no, no, you don't understand,"

Gladys said. "What I mean is I think he's developed a thing for . . . fruits."

"A man's diet is his own business," I said. "I'm partial to pears myself."

Gladys rolled her eyes and sighed. Suddenly, I understood what it was she was trying to tell me and I didn't like it one bit. Jack a sissy? There wasn't a chance in hell. Jack was the straightest guy I ever knew. Guys who swore as much as Jack and who liked to play with guns as much as Jack couldn't possibly be that way. Everybody knew that.

Once Gladys saw my reaction to the news, she shrugged wearily and put her head against my shoulder.

"Look, Gladys," I said, "I'm not saying you're lying, but all this is a little hard to believe. Jack and I go way back. I know him better than I know my own brother."

"I thought you were an only child."

"Never mind that," I said. "What makes you think Jack's turned . . . sissy?"

"He's living in Beverly Hills, in a hairdresser's guesthouse," she said. "I've heard they're awfully chummy, Jack and his new friend Armando. Armando Eclair."

"Armando?" I said, trying to imagine a guy like Jack hanging out with someone named Armando. All this was hitting me pretty hard. Jack, the guy who'd saved my life, the guy who'd have given me his right arm even though I already had a right arm and didn't need two of them, the guy who liked to pinch dames and shoot rifles, the guy whose idea of a fun evening was to go out and beat up dope dealers, that Jack hanging out with a Beverly Hills hairdresser named Armando?

"Can you tell me when all this started?" I asked. "Was Jack on a case at the time?"

"Yeah," she said. "He told me a little about it at first. Some farm couple from Indiana had hired him to find their runaway daughter. A sixteen year old. She was a 'working girl.'"

"I see," I said. "And what sort of work did she do exactly?"

Gladys rolled her eyes for some reason. "She was a hooker," she said impatiently. "A whore, a prostitute. She did it for money."

"I never met a hooker who did it for cornmeal," I said. "Of course she did it for money. I wasn't born yesterday, you know. I've been around the block a few thousand times myself."

"That's nice," Gladys said. "They say walking is the best exercise."

"Listen, Gladys," I said calmly, suddenly realizing that her poor troubled mind was skating on thin ice. "I'm sure there's a good explanation for all this. Have you talked to Jack's partner, Quinn?"

"Quinn's been on vacation ever since all this started," she said, still sniffling.

"Okay," I said decisively. "I'm going over to Beverly Hills to have a little man-to-man heart-to-heart tête-à-tête with old Jack. If he doesn't come up with a little straight talk for his old buddy, I'll beat some sense into him. Now let's have one of your million-dollar smiles."

Try as she might, the best old Gladys could come up with was a fifty-dollar smirk, but I patted her lightly on the cheek, grabbed my jacket and my fedora, and went out into the somber Los Angeles twilight to see what was what.

Even though I hadn't been to the Coast in just under thirty years, I was amazed at how naturally I knew my way around. It was as if the rental heap was driving itself. Instinctively, I drove several blocks west, took Coldwater Canyon into the hills and then back down, and before I knew it I was driving past some of the most lavishly gaudy estates known to man—all of them in a different style of architecture, all of them with the mandatory Rollses, Mercedes, and Jags parked in their driveways. In Hollywood, they say, you are what you drive. That made me something between a wreck and a junker, but I didn't give a damn.

While the scenery sped past, I tried to get a fix on Gladys's little speech about Jack, and figure out what the hell I was going to say to him if what she'd said was even remotely true. Deep down, though, I knew Jack must've had something up his sleeve, something that was part of a case, something that was so big he couldn't even risk telling Gladys what it was all about. That had to be it—there was no other possible explanation.

Armando the hairdresser must have been having some kind of a shindig, because when I pulled up to the street he lived on, all the available parking had been taken and a gaggle of uniformed valets was running around parking and unparking the forty or so Mercedes, Rollses, and Jags that had pulled up in the drive. Back in my day, a hairdresser was a dame who lived in a walk-up flat, colored her nails purple, dyed her hair with peroxide, and chewed gum like she was getting paid for it by the hour. But this Armando mug must've been another story. The pad he owned was a Tudor castle minus the drawbridge and moat. Off the top of my head, I figured it was worth at least a cool million if not more. No matter how many haircuts he gave, I couldn't figure out how a sissy barber could possibly put together enough dough to buy a joint like this one.

Anyway, knowing that the valets wouldn't want to soil their uniforms on the cheap vinyl seats of my rental heap, I drove around the block about four times until I found a free space. The fact that the guy was having a party was actually a blessing in disguise, because it meant I could sneak onto the estate grounds unseen and have my little chat with old Jack without having to put up with this Armando Eclair character hanging around the whole time.

With that as my plan, I locked the heap, walked the three blocks back to the house, and sashayed into the front foyer with a bevy of other guests. As soon as I was in I looked around. The usual Hollywood movers and shakers were there—agents, producers, directors, a few starlet types. A small crowd, including the movie star Rita Klondyke, had gathered around a turbanned dame who seemed to be reading palms. I didn't spot Jack in the crowd right away, so I grabbed a drink off a butler's tray and mingled. As I innocently stalked around the room, I kept hearing the same phrase over and over, wherever I went. The phrase must have been a biggie in Hollywood. It was "Let's have lunch."

Somehow, I managed to meander outside to where the pool and cabana were located. Since Gladys had said Jack was staying in the guesthouse, I headed in that direction. It was a tiny little bungalow, stucco Spanish style, with a pink awning suspended over the French doors. The lights were out inside.

Lucky for me there were no party guests outside, probably because a dry chill had settled in with the sunset a few hours ago. I put my cocktail down, lit a cigarette to calm my nerves, and knocked lightly on Jack's door. There was no answer, but I figured if Jack was sleeping I'd wake him up, since this was pretty important. So I knocked again, louder this time.

My second knock got a response, but it wasn't the kind of response I'd expected. It was a gunshot, and it penetrated the quiet around me as if someone had stuck a firecracker in my ear.

I reacted instinctively, wrapped my hand in my jacket, bashed the door window in, and unlocked the bolt from the inside. I would have been in in an instant, but the chain lock caught me by surprise and held me up just long enough for whoever was inside to make a getaway through the back. I tried to circle around the house, but my rolled up jacket had caught on the inside door latch, and by the time I wrestled my hand free it was too late. Whoever had been there was long gone. My one hope was that Jack had been the shooter and not the shootee.

I circled around again, busted the chain lock with a solid kick to the center of the door, and went in. It was pitch black inside, so I switched on a dim table lamp in the living-room area which provided just enough illumination to keep me from tripping over the furniture.

"Are you there, Jack?" I whispered. "It's me, Slade."

There was no answer, so I wandered into the hallway. The place was plenty dark and eerily quiet. I'd read enough mystery novels and seen enough Hitchcock movies in my day to know that this could only mean one thing—trouble was lurking somewhere, probably just around the next corner.

But it wasn't. I searched Jack's bedroom, his kitchen, his bathroom, even under the bed, but I found nothing—no corpse, no ambusher waiting in the shadows to jump me. *Nada.* It was strange as hell but someone had shot off a gun, heard me rustling in the bushes outside, and taken a powder.

I decided I'd wait old Jack out, so I settled down on his couch and leafed through a few old *National Geographics.* I was midway into a fascinating article about fertility rites among the Burpee Indians of Borneo when I heard someone at the door. I grabbed my gat and held it ready under the magazine—just in case.

The intruder knocked a few times, then let himself in. I knew right away it was Armando. I could tell by his hairdo, a blond bob with a curl in the middle of his forehead that looked like it had been glued down with epoxy. He had a pencil-thin mustache that looked like it had been drawn on his face, and finely sculpted features. If he'd been a dame he would've been a cute one.

"And who might *you* be?" he asked in that uppity manner people sometimes affect when strangers are sitting on their property.

"I *might* be anybody," I said. "I *might* be Ginger Rogers. On the other hand, I *might* be Doris Day."

"Whoever you are," he said limply, "one

thing's for sure. You're definitely *not* a professional comedian."

"The name's Slade," I said. "Mac Slade. I'm a dick."

By the suddenly friendly look on Armando's face, I knew right away I'd made a poor choice of words in describing my occupation. Just for the hell of it, I took out my wallet and flashed my shield at him.

"I'm *very* impressed that you own a wallet," he said finally, "but the fact is you happen to be trespassing on private property, dear boy."

"I'm not your dear boy, pal," I said. "I happen to be waiting for Jack. I'm an old friend. From the War."

This seemed to clear the air for him. "You must mean Jacques," he said.

"*Jacques?*" I said, startled at the thought that old mean Jack might have adopted a frog name.

"Funny," he mused. "Jacques never mentioned that he was in the War. Which war was it?"

"The Korean War," I said. "We were stationed in Sicily."

"Well, any friend of Jacques' is a friend of mine," he said. "Can I get you a beer?"

"As a matter of fact," I said, "you can."

Smiling, he pranced over to the refrigerator, which was directly behind the couch I was sitting on. He started to say something about Jack's plentiful beer supply, most of which I didn't catch, but he never had a chance to finish the sentence. There was a silence for a few seconds, then what sounded like a gasp, then a bloodcurdling scream that was louder and more chilling than the loudest female yelp I'd ever heard, and next the poor dumb fruitcake was on the floor, out cold.

I got up to see what the brouhaha was all about and when my eyes landed on what had scared Armando, tough bastard that I am, I almost repeated the pansy's little scenario verbatim.

Jack was curled up in the refrigerator, dead as can be.

❑

The sight of my old pal Jack with his head leaning against a jar of Weight Watchers mayonnaise and his feet propped up against a tub of Smucker's orange preserves made me sick to my stomach. My knees grew weak and tears welled up in my eyes. I sunk to the floor and quivered for a few minutes before anger began to burst through the grief. It was the intense rage of revenge, and I vowed there and then to get the guy who'd gotten Jack. The anger that welled up within me made my hands tremble, but I lifted myself off the floor and pulled myself together. I had work to do. The cops would no doubt be there any minute—I was sure Armando's glass-shattering scream must have been heard in the main house—and if I was going to pinch the guy that did this to Jack, I had to get the evidence before the coppers did.

Armando was still out cold on the linoleum, so I examined Jack's body to get a fix on the murderer's modus operandi. From what I could gather, Jack had been strangled with a piano wire—high C, I think—stuffed in the fridge, then finished off with a .38 in the head. That had been the gunshot I'd heard when I'd been nosing around. For some reason, the murderer hadn't wanted Jack's body to be detected for a few days—thus the refrigerator business. If I hadn't come around, and if Armando hadn't offered me a beer, God only knows how long Jack would have stayed in there.

After I'd gotten enough poop on the state of Jack's body, I rifled his pockets and went through his wallet. I only found one little item of interest—a parking stub from a joint in Hollywood called Al Greco's House of Massage. I stuck it in my own wallet and replaced Jack's in his back pocket. Then I turned away—I couldn't stand to look at him for another second—pain, grief, and anger were getting the better of me. But before closing the fridge door, I reached over between Jack's right arm and left leg and grabbed a can of Bud, popped it open, and guzzled it in one gulp. I needed the fortification.

Armando started to gradually come to, letting out a falsetto moan that sounded like a chipmunk in heat. I wanted him conscious to question him before the coppers arrived, so I searched Jack's place for smelling salts. I didn't find any, but I did locate the next best thing—an old sweat sock in Jack's laundry hamper. I stuck it under Armando's thin, sculptured nose and within a millisecond, the guy was awake with a grimace on his kisser.

"What happened?" he asked as soon as he'd focussed on me. "Did I faint?"

"No," I said. "You wanted to show me your impersonation of a dust mop. Yeah, of course you fainted. You saw something in the refrigerator that didn't belong there. Remember?"

As the vision returned to his consciousness, I thought he was going to pass out again. His eyes rolled in his head for a second, but he must have caught himself before blacking out.

"Jacques!" he exclaimed. "Jacques is—"

"You got it," I said. "Strangled, shot, and left for dead in his goddamn refrigerator." The anger was returning and my hand started to tremble again.

"Oh, my," he said, putting the back of his hand to his mouth to stifle a gasp. "Who would want to do a nasty thing like that to Jacques?"

"That's just want I wanted to ask *you,*" I said, eyeing the little rodent suspiciously. He caught the drift.

"Surely you don't suspect *me*?" he said, suddenly afraid. "I was in the main house, entertaining all night. I had guests. It would have been the epitome of rudeness for me to have excused myself to put Jacques in the refrigerator. What would I have said, 'Pardon me, I have to put someone in the fridge'? Besides, I had nothing against Jacques—he always paid his rent on time."

"What prompted you to come down here then?" I asked.

"I saw a light on and wanted to tell Jacques to join us inside, at the party. I hate a party pooper, don't you?"

I looked him over from head to toe and came to the conclusion that he wouldn't have even been able to lift a guy of Jack's weight, let alone stick him in the fridge. And I knew Jack well enough to know that he wouldn't have volunteered to go in by himself.

"Did Jack have any enemies?" I asked.

"None that I know of," Armando said. "Everybody loved Jacques."

"Well, somebody sure as hell didn't," I said. "And you can count on one thing, pal. I'm going to get revenge. I'm going to personally pinch the guy who did this to Jack!"

"You call *that* revenge! Pinching?" he said. "Shooting is revenge! Strangling is revenge! Pinching is what you do to boys with cute buns."

I was tempted to slug the little wimp, but I didn't get the opportunity because the moment he'd finished jabbering, the door burst open and a plainclothes police dick was standing in the doorway with his gat out and his fly open.

"All right," he said uncertainly, "what's the fuss all about here? Somebody said they heard a scream."

I gave the guy the once-over and rolled

my eyes. He couldn't have been over thirty-two, but he looked like he was closer to sixteen, one of those college-educated detectives who don't know their ass from a hole in the ground because they lack street experience. He had two beat cops behind him and they entered the room and started pawing everything like a couple of imbeciles.

"I wouldn't touch anything if I were you," I said. "You might muss up the prints."

"Don't touch the prints," the young detective said. "That includes lithographs, etchings, and silk screens. Did I leave anything out?"

"There's a woodcut in the bathroom," Armando offered.

"I meant *fingerprints,* you morons," I said.

The young dick furrowed his brow. All this was clearly going over his head. In fact, I saw it go over his head and land on the upper door hinge behind him.

"What do we need fingerprints for?" he asked, putting his gat away. "This doesn't look like anything more than a little domestic squabble. A lover's quarrel. Am I right?"

The implication ticked me off and I

looked first at Armando in disgust and then at the young cop with something resembling rage.

"Look, Junior," I said as patiently as I could, "let me acquaint you with the situation here. My name is Mac Slade. I'm a private dick out of New York. This guy here is Armando Eclair—he owns this pad and this guesthouse. The guy curled up in the fridge, whom you haven't met yet, is an old friend of mine from the War named Jack Mushnik . . ."

"Thanks for the intro," the guy said. "I'm Lieutenant Lou Tennant of the LAPD. Homicide Division. Ordinarily, they wouldn't have sent a homicide person on a domestic call, but everybody else was busy so—" Suddenly, he turned pale and a look that was slightly dumber than his regular look fell over his face. "What guy in the refrigerator?" he asked.

I sighed and rolled my eyes. The guy was kind of slow on the uptake. "You want me to draw you a picture?" I asked.

"Yeah," he said, handing me a pad and pencil from his breast pocket.

Sighing, I whipped off a quick sketch of Jack curled up in the fridge and handed it back to him. Then he nodded for one of his flunkies to open the fridge door. A look of shock came over the young dick as he looked first at the sight of my old buddy curled up between the mayo and the jam, then down at my drawing, and back again at the real-life scenario. It was a few moments until he opened his trap.

"Not a bad likeness," he said, waving the sketch. "You've got talent, that's for sure. The shadowing and general composition are excellent."

Half a second later, he fainted.

❑

"I'm sorry," he said, after I'd revived him with Jack's old sweat sock. "It's my first real case. I've never seen an actual corpse before."

I helped him to his feet. He cleared his throat, hunched his shoulders together like a tough guy, and pulled his gat on me. The reality of the situation was finally sinking in.

"You can put the roscoe away," I said. "You won't need it."

His brow wrinkled quizzically. "I'm sorry," he said, "but what's a roscoe?"

"The gat," I said. "Put the gat away."

"Gat?" he said. "Are you an American citizen, Slade?"

"The *gun*, the *piece*, the *pistol*!" I said,

irritated. "It's dick slang. You'll pick it up after you've been around for awhile."

He nodded and put the police special back in its holster. "Okay, men," he said to his boys, "search the place for clues."

I shook my head. "I hate to intrude, Junior," I said, "but don't you think it might be a good idea to dust before you start handling everything?"

"Right," he said. "I want you men to dust first. And make sure you get in all the little nooks and crannies. When you're done, clean the windows, lightly mop the floors, and shake out the rugs."

"For *fingerprints*!" I shouted at him.

"Right," he said. "And make sure you clean up all the fingerprints, especially the ones on the glass."

I wondered exactly which college this dimwit had gotten his degree from, but somehow I managed to hold on to the thin thread of my patience. After all, he was a police dick and if I was going to solve this case and get my revenge on Jack's killer, it'd help to have him as an ally, dense as he was. At least he'd have access to records and files that might come in handy.

With that in mind, I took him aside and whispered in his ear the set of instructions he had to give to his men, which included interviewing all the party guests individually and cross-checking everybody's alibi. He nodded, thanked me, and barked out the orders like an old pro. He was an okay guy really—he just needed a little experience in the field.

While the police work was going on, I took Armando aside, told him to tell his guests—who had gathered in a large knot in front of the guesthouse door—to stay put for interrogation. Then, while I sat down on Jack's sofa and smoked a cigarette, I had Armando draw up a full guest list of the evening's party. Everybody was a suspect, I told him. Everybody.

Finally, I left. I had loads of work to do. I told Lieutenant Tennant that we'd be in touch. I didn't tell Armando we'd be in touch because I figured he'd take it the wrong way. On the way to my car, I asked one of the valets if he'd seen anyone trying to leave in a hurry around the approximate time of the murder. He thought about it for a second, but came up blank. Then the bastard had the nerve to ask me for a tip.

"You want a tip, *amigo*?" I asked.

"*Si, si,*" he said.

"Plant corn early."

And at that, I was off.

Even though I tore out of my Beverly Hills parking space with a screech of tires, I really had no idea where I was going at first. It was getting late and jet lag was starting to overtake me, but I had plenty to do before slumber time; for starters, I had to give Gladys the bad news—never my favorite chore. Then I had to find a motel room somewhere, and, most important of all, before the cops ransacked the place for clues, I wanted to check Jack's office for information regarding the runaway case he'd been working on.

I drove around the block four times before deciding to handle the worst of the chores first. Like a schmuck, I'd promised Tennant that I'd break the news of Jack's death to Gladys. After all, I didn't want her reading about it in the papers tomorrow morning, and I certainly didn't want a nincompoop like the lieutenant handling it.

Gladys was asleep when I got there, so I woke her up gently, handed her a robe, fixed her a tall glass of brandy, and sat her down on the couch. Then I gave her the bad news, gently, and held her shaking body as she wept. All things considered, she took it pretty well—after all, Jack was a dick and danger came with the territory. Gladys knew that as well as anybody and I think she'd been psychologically prepared for years. When I was certain she'd be all right, I told her about my plan to get revenge on Jack's killer if it was the last thing I ever did. Then I put her back to bed and went on my way.

She'd given me the keys to Jack's office, so I headed my rental heap toward Hollywood Boulevard. Even though it was late, the local slime was out in full force and the street was littered with lowlifes of all description—bikers, punks, and, worst of all, street mimes. A group of Hell's Angels was camped in front of Jack's office door and I had to push my way through them to gain entrance. If one of them had said boo, I would have punched his face in. I was in that kind of mood.

I had to go through a song and a dance for the security guard in the lobby reception area, but once I assured him I was a copper and flashed my badge quick enough so he couldn't get a real fix on it, the old codger let me go. I found Jack's office at the end of the hall on the fifth floor and let myself in.

It looked just like my office—a mess, only worse since Jack obviously hadn't been using it much lately. A slice of pizza had bonded itself to his desk and there were old *Racing Forms* and half-empty bottles of rye all over the place. Jack's copy of *Henderson's Remedial Guide to Effective Detective Work* lay half open on a chair, the chapter called "How to Slug a Dame for Maximum Effect," dog-eared and underlined. I took a few swigs from an open rye bottle, and unlocked Jack's file cabinet.

It didn't take me long to find what I was looking for, mainly because there was only one file in the cabinet and it was the right one. It was labeled "Krause, Gilda," but except for a snapshot of the sixteen-year-old runaway stapled to the outside of the file folder, it was empty. Strange, I thought, since Jack was a pretty meticulous note maker. I searched around for a few more minutes, but didn't turn up a thing from the Krause file. My business there was done and I was just about to put the snapshot in my wallet when I heard a voice coming from behind me.

"Hold it right there, mac," the intruder said.

❑

I raised my hands and turned around slowly, more out of curiosity than fear. My assailant was a dame—I'd known that from the voice—and she was holding a gun on me in the modern police way—arms outstretched, knees bent slightly, eyes staring straight ahead—and I could tell that, whoever she was, she meant business. A lump formed in my throat while I studied her in the half-darkness. She was a knockout with long tanned legs, silky blond tresses and the kind of body that could put a mug like me in the intensive care unit.

"Okay," she said very businesslike, "now move over two feet toward the corner so I can get a look at you. And don't try any funny stuff."

"No funny stuff?" I asked, obeying her

order. "Aw gee. And here I was planning to break into my Mr. Rogers impersonation."

"I wouldn't be so casual if I were you," she said, still holding the gun on me in that peculiar TV-cop way. "Breaking and entering happens to be a felony in this state."

"I'm guilty of entering," I said. "But I haven't broken anything. Even the vases are intact."

"You must be a dick," she said. "Only a dick would make a dumb crack like that."

"You win the kewpie doll, sweetheart," I said. "The name's Slade—Mac Slade. Private dick out of New York."

At that, she sighed more out of relief than impatience and lowered her bazooka.

"You're a cool one," I said. "Don't you even want to see any identification? Don't you even want to search me?" Boy, did I want this dame to search me. For about three hours or so. "For your information," I said, "I happen to be carrying a rod."

She shrugged. "So what? There's no fishing around here for miles. Besides, I recognize you from a picture Jack once showed me."

Now I was confused. Who was this dame—one of Jack's girl friends? A bimbo he kept on the side? She must have detected my puzzlement. "I'm J.C. Quinn," she said. "Jack's partner."

That one threw me for a loop. J.C. Quinn a dame!? Old Jack was never the kind of guy who'd take a dame for a partner, though I had to admit looking at Quinn's kisser everyday sure beat looking into the mug of some guy with a five o'clock shadow.

I couldn't help but laugh. "You gotta be kidding me, lady," I said. "A dame dick? Jack would never have hired a broad."

This must have got her dandruff up because I saw her lips tighten and her smile fade. "For one thing," she said, "I'm not a dame and I'm not a broad. I'm a woman."

I didn't see the difference, but I kept my yap shut.

"And furthermore," she continued, "I can shoot as well as a man, punch as well as a man, put together clues as well as a man, and beat up dope dealers as well as a man. The only thing I can't do as well as a man is pee standing up."

"I'm not too good at that myself," I admitted. She was some tough cookie all right, beautiful, smart, and hard as a rock. Still, I couldn't help but wonder what she was doing in the office at this time of night, especially considering the fact that she was supposed to be out of town.

"I thought you were supposed to be on vacation," I said.

"I was. I flew back a few hours ago when they told me about Jack. Poor old Jack."

"When *who* told you about Jack?" I asked, suspiciously.

She smiled condescendingly. "I got a few friends in the precinct, Slade," she said. "There isn't much that goes on in this town that I don't know about sooner or later."

"Well, don't trouble yourself, lady," I said. "I'm looking into it and I'll get my hands on the mug that got Jack in no time. And when I do, he's as good as dead. You can bet on it."

"Don't *trouble* myself!" she bellowed. "*I* was Jack's partner. *I'll* get the mug who got Jack, and when I do he'll wish he was never born."

She'd spit the words at me—"trouble" and "I'll"—and they'd landed on my chin.

"Forget it," I said. "I've got dibs on the murderer. I was here first. It's just your tough luck, sweetheart."

"We'll see about that," she said angrily. On that note, she stuck her gat back in her holster, turned sharply on her three-inch heels, and walked out, slamming the door behind her with such force it made the glass rattle.

❑

So it was going to be a race—a fifty-yard dash to see who would be the first to exact revenge from Jack's killer, a detective's relay with the prize being the head of a murderer. Naturally, Quinn wouldn't have a chance, not against the likes of me, but I had to respect her spunk. I like dames with spunk. I like them even more if their measurements are as good as Quinn's.

After her exit, I stuck the Krause broad's picture in my wallet, and tooled around the seamier side of Hollywood looking for an inn with a vacancy. Most of them, to my surprise, were filled up. Must have been a scumbag convention in town or something. But I needed some shut-eye pretty bad, so I kept looking and finally found a joint off Hollywood Boulevard, a real tourist's dream called the Hi-Ho Motel. The neon sign outside alternated between flashing the word "Vacancy," and the phrase, "Radios in Every Room." Wow, a radio. What a luxury.

I registered, schlepped my poor tired body around a few corridors to my room, and fell into bed. But it was no good. Try as I might, I couldn't seem to relax enough to sleep. The walls were paper thin and the couple in the next room were doing the horizontal mambo like it was going out of style. The moans and groans aroused me just enough to keep me from dozing. Finally, I gave up, slapped on my clothes, and went out to my heap.

I'd decided to pay a call on Al Greco's House of Massage, which, as luck would have it, was no more than five blocks from my motel room. It didn't take any kind of genius to figure out that Gilda Krause, the runaway, worked there, and as long as I wasn't getting any shut-eye, I might as well see what she had to say.

Al Greco's House of Massage was the usual windowless hole-in-the-wall den of iniquity with badly drawn pictures of half-naked broads on its stucco walls and a neon sign that was missing more than half its letters. I patted my gat to make sure it was there, tilted my fedora over one eye, and went in.

The waiting room was empty except for a weasly little guy with slits for eyes sitting behind a reception counter and thumbing listlessly through a girlie magazine. He had a two-day growth of beard and puffs of body hair rose above the shoulder straps of his dirty T-shirt. His teeth looked like they hadn't been cleaned since the Harding administration.

I banged on the counter to get his attention.

"Help ya?" he asked.

"Maybe," I said. I dug in my wallet and handed him the snapshot of Gilda Krause. "She work here?"

He didn't even look at the photo. "It'll cost ya a fin," was all he said, turning back to his girlie rag.

"I don't have a Finn," I said, "but I can give you a Swede, a Norwegian, or a Czech."

I guess he didn't have a sense of humor because he just stared at me with those beady little slit-eyes. "Don't take checks," he said. "Mastercard, Diners Club, and Visa, but no checks."

I wasn't in the mood for wiseguys. "Look, you little sleazebag piece of street trash," I said, grabbing his T-shirt in my hairy paw and pulling his little rodent face so close to mine I could see each strand of his nose hair. "Does this broad work here or not?"

"Yeah, yeah," he said, his face red with fear. "She works here. Monday, Wednesday, and Friday. Tonight's her night off."

"You wouldn't be pulling my leg would

ya, sport?" I asked, tightening my grip on his shirt. "I'm not in the mood for wiseguys tonight."

"It's her night off," he said. "I swear it!"

"Then give me her home address." I let him back down, and with trembling hands he wrote down Gilda Krause's address and handed it over. Then he reached under the counter, probably for a billy club or a gun, but I caught him in time, and smashed his right hand with the butt of my own trusty roscoe. He yelped with pain and pulled his hand to his chest.

"Try that again, buster," I said. "Go ahead. Reach for it. Make my day."

But he didn't budge. He just turned back to his girlie magazine as if I wasn't there anymore.

I stuck my gat back in its shoulder holster, turned on my heels, and made for the door. Just as I was about to exit, a guy about the size of a construction crane comes barreling into the joint, knocking me into one of the waiting-room chairs with the force of his entrance. I would have decked the bastard for rudeness, but he looked like he had something on his mind, and besides, as I said, he was bigger than me. About four times bigger.

The weasly guy at the desk got a chuckle

or two out of the fact that I'd been knocked on my keister, but his grin faded as soon as he saw that the human brontosaurus was headed his way with trouble written all over his kisser in red ink.

"Where's Peaches?" the behemoth said. "Peaches Moskowitz?"

Like the nitwit that he was, the weasel shrugged and said, "I dunno."

"You want I should shake the information outa ya?" the giant said.

"I never heard of a Peaches Moskowitz," the weasel claimed, scared out of his wits, the little he had. "I swear it!"

But the big guy wasn't the patient type. He grabbed the weasel by the shirt, lifted him up, and started to shake him like he'd promised until information came spilling out of his pockets.

"Where is she?" the human Mack truck bellowed. "Where's my Peaches?"

"I tell ya I dunno!" the wimp said.

Finally, the big guy got fed up and threw the weasel against the back wall like a kid would throw a rag doll away. The weasel slumped to the floor, unconscious.

While all this was going on, I'd been sitting in the waiting-room chair watching with rapt fascination, hoping that King Kong wouldn't take notice of me. Just to be safe, I kept my hand near my gat, even though I had the distinct feeling that six slugs from a .38 would irritate him about as much as a case of hemmorhoids would bother a person of average size.

Once the weasel had become something less than scintillating company, the big guy tore his way down a curtained-off corridor and peeked into each of the little massage cubicles, a procedure that produced a scream here and there followed by the behemoth's grunt of displeasure. Clearly, Peaches Moskowitz was not around, but the big guy wasn't giving up. By the time he'd reached the end of the corridor, I'd gotten up from my seat to peek behind the curtain, just to see what he was up to. It was just simple curiosity on my part, no more, no less.

He was rapping on a door labeled "Private," at the end of the hallway, and he was rapping so hard that the power of his fist finally caused the door to fly open. I saw him go into what must have been the manager's office and, as soon as he'd slammed the door shut behind him, I snuck down the corridor and listened to what was going on inside.

After the manager had gone through a few standard pleas like "What's the meaning of this?" and "Get out of here or I'll call the police," Godzilla told him to shut up and sit down. There was a moment of silence before the big guy spoke.

"I wanna talk to Peaches," he said firmly.

"Try a grocery store," the manager said. "They might even let you talk to nectarines."

The big guy wasn't amused. Anybody who's ever tried to get a laugh out of a charging Brahma bull by telling it one-liners could have predicted that.

"Peaches Moskowitz," Dumbo said flatly. "She used ta work here when dis place was a striptease joint ten years ago. Where is she?"

"Look," the manager said, not realizing that he was dealing with a gorilla that didn't take no for an answer. "I never heard of a Peaches Lefkowitz. Now, please . . ."

I put my ear closer to the door and what I heard sounded like a struggle, a struggle that I was certain the manager would lose. I figured the big guy had probably grabbed him by the lapels and was trying to shake information out of him, just as he'd done a few minutes before with the weasel.

"I'm . . . telling you . . . the truth," the

manager said, and it sounded like he was gasping for air. "I bought the place from a guy . . . Clyde Griswald . . . ten years ago. . . ."

Then there was another moment of silence, an eerie silence. It didn't last long though. Within seconds, another struggle erupted. Curiosity got the better of me and I peered through the keyhole, but just as I'd focussed on the wrestling match inside, a gunshot rang out and the door flew open in my kisser, flattening my nose into my face.

Blood trickled down my chin, but I'd had my nose busted enough times not to care. Hidden behind the door, I saw the big guy race past me for the front door and exit. Inside the office, the manager was slumped at his desk. A small puddle of blood was forming on his blotter. I lifted his head up slightly and saw what had finally silenced him—a bullet square between his eyes.

The gunshot had caused a good deal of commotion in the curtained-off cubicles, and a couple of the girls had emerged half-dressed from their rooms to see what was up. I knew the cops would be there as soon as one of the employees got to the pay phone, so, not wanting to be caught at the scene of the crime twice in one night, I stuck a Kleenex in my throbbing proboscis, found an open window in the rear of the joint, and dashed out of there toot sweet.

On the way back to my motel room, I bought a fifth of rye. The noise from the next room had died down and I had myself about four or five glasses of the rotgut before I finally dozed off.

The bright Los Angeles sun and the resumption of activity in the next room woke me the next morning at about seven o'clock. Jet lag and booze had combined to give me a hangover. My head felt like it was made out of marble and my stomach was making noises that sounded like water going through clogged plumbing.

I grabbed some breakfast at a greasy

spoon down the block. While I shoveled in an omelet, three cups of coffee, and a rasher of undercooked bacon, I went over the twenty names on Armando's guest list. As far as I was concerned, everybody on the list was a prime suspect, but there were too many of them and I had no idea where to start. Interviewing all twenty of them would take me the better part of a week and I didn't have that much time to spare, not with Quinn hot on the case. So I decided to pay a call on Lieutenant Lou Tennant to see if he could narrow the list down to three or four likely choices.

I found him with his feet propped up on his desk, snoozing. Like me, he must've slept in his duds because they were about as wrinkled as mine. The bags under his eyes were a matching set of luggage that could've held enough clothes for a two-week vacation in Maui.

I cleared my throat loudly and he sprang awake as suddenly as if someone had stuck a handshake buzzer in his butt.

"You look beat," I said, taking off my hat and sitting down. "Rough night?"

"Rough is putting it mildly," he said. "After finishing the job over in Beverly Hills, I got a call on a homicide over in Hollywood. Manager of a massage parlor. I was up all night."

"I might be able to help you on that one," I said, pausing for effect before dropping the bombshell. "I was there."

That got his attention. He bolted up straight as a board and his eyes widened like a dog about to get a T-bone.

"You mean you were a material witness?" he asked.

"Not really," I said. "I saw who did it, but I don't know squat about fabrics. Offhand, I'd say the perpetrator was wearing gabardine, but it could've been 100 percent wool for all I know."

"That'll do," he said, excitedly. "Who did it?"

I put up my palm to calm him down a little. "Hold your horses, Junior," I said. "I'll scratch your back if you scratch mine."

"Are you trying to make a deal with me, Slade?" he asked. The guy was real swift on the uptake.

"You got it."

"I could slap you with a subpoena, you know?" he said confidently.

I shrugged. "Go ahead."

At that, he reached into his desk drawer, pulled out a subpoena, and belted me across the face with it.

"Now that that's over with," I said, "do we do business or don't we?"

"Depends on what you want," he said.

"Nothing much," I said, handing him Armando's guest list. "Just a lead on some of these names and access to anything you find out about the Mushnik murder."

"You drive a hard bargain, Slade," he said.

I shrugged. "A man's gotta do what a man's gotta do," I said. "Now do we deal or do I take a walk?"

He thought about it for a second, then nodded. "Okay, you win," he said. "It's not kosher, but I'll do what I can. But first, tell me what you know about the massage parlor thing."

"The killer was a big guy—maybe six eight or so, built like a Sherman tank, but not as friendly. White. Caucasian."

"Caucasian, huh?" Tennant said. "What's a Caucasian doing in this part of the country?"

"You got me there, Lieutenant," I said. "Anyway, he came in around midnight looking for a dame named Peaches Moskowitz. The manager of the joint tried to plug him, the big guy took the gun away, and the rest is history."

"Would you be willing to take a look

at some mug shots?" Tennant asked. I nodded and he tossed a book in front of me. It was a standard police mug-shot book, filled with photos of beer steins from around the world. I leafed through it but didn't see any mugs I recognized.

"Try this one," Tennant said.

Sighing, I did as he asked, turning page after page until I found the mug we were both looking for. "That's the one," I said, pointing to a photo of the human moving van I'd seen the night before at Al Greco's.

Tennant looked at the picture. "Moose Lebowitz," he said. "Alias Earl Salvador, alias Johnny Mopp, alias Machine Gun Pfiffelmeister, alias Jack Hammer. Did a stretch in Folsom in the sixties. Broke out in '69."

"Broke out, eh?" I said. "With what—acne?"

"Psoriasis and eczema, I think," Tennant said.

"Convicted of murder in '74, did ten years at San Quentin, just got out on parole. I remember reading about the case in college. During the murder trial, he claimed he'd been set up by his girl friend, that Peaches Moskowitz woman, a stripper-hooker type."

"Fascinating," I said impatiently. "All

you have to do is find this Moskowitz dame and you'll probably be able to nab the big guy."

But Tennant was shaking his head. "I'm afraid it's not that simple," he said. "Peaches Moskowitz is dead. Drug overdose nine years ago. She free-based Lomotil and Actifed."

"Tough luck," I said. "Guess you'll just have to put out an APB on the guy."

Tennant nodded and closed the mug-shot book. "Now," he said, "what can I do for you?"

"For starters, you can tell me who's who on this guest list," I said.

Tennant snatched it off the desk and looked it over. "We did a few cursory interviews last night," he said. "Most of the names on the list had pretty good alibis. We're still trying to corroborate a few of the stories. I'd planned to question about four of them again—Rita Klondyke, Marty Kahn, Elvira Swann, and that hairdresser fellow, Armando Eclair."

"Can you give me a quick rundown on the four?" I asked.

"Rita Klondyke, I assume you know about. She's a big star. The Swann dame is a psychic/astrologer type with a lot of celebrity clients. Pretty flakey. Kahn is a high-powered agent, also with plenty of celebrity clients. Armando you've already met."

"What can you tell me about J.C. Quinn?" I asked.

"Jack's partner?" Tennant asked, somewhat nonplussed. I nodded. "You don't suspect *her*, do you?"

"I suspect everybody," I said. "Standard procedure. I haven't figured motive out yet, but she sure got back to town fast. A little too fast."

"As far as I know, her record is clean," Tennant said. "She's been a dick for about ten years, majored in criminology at UCLA with a minor in Home Ec. She's good with a gun, tough with her fists, and she's built like a—"

"I know, I know," I said, imagining her gorgeous body in my mind. In fact, both of us sat there daydreaming about it for a good twenty seconds before I finally got up to leave.

"I'll see ya around, Lou," I said. "Thanks for the poop."

"Hold it a minute, Slade," he said, stopping me. "I know you're an experienced dick and all that, I know your middle name is danger—"

"Actually, it's Claude," I said, "but don't spread it around."

"Anyway," Tennant continued, "I know you're going to resent this, but for your own safety, I'm afraid I'm going to have to put a police tail on you."

"Yeah?" I said. "And what if I give him the slip?"

Tennant shrugged. "You can try," he said, "but I doubt if he'll accept it. Most of my men don't wear slips."

I didn't bother to explain. I just let out with a weary sigh, shook my head, and left the room.

❑

Gilda Krause's apartment was an old stucco affair in a marginal section of East Los Angeles, not too far from Los Feliz. Burned palms lined the street and the curbside grass hadn't been watered for years. It was the kind of neighborhood that featured a lot of souped-up Chevys, some of them parked on front lawns, and there was graffiti everywhere—on the buildings, on the sidewalks, even on the neighborhood pets.

I parked my rental heap in the only available space, a few blocks away from the address the weasel had given me the night before, and walked the two blocks to the Krause girl's house. I hadn't gone more than twelve paces when who should exit the Krause building but my old pal Moose Lebowitz. I ducked behind one of the rotting palms that lined the sidewalk and watched as he barreled out of the apartment building and into a '78 Cadillac parked right outside. With a screech of rubber that could easily be heard ten miles away, he was off.

As soon as he was out of sight, I ran for the building, hurriedly found Gilda Krause's apartment number on the mailboxes, picked the front door lock, and tore up the stairs to the second floor. I prayed that the Krause girl was alive and breathing, but I doubted it. Moose Lebowitz didn't strike me as the type of guy that left people alive and breathing.

A stereo was blaring from inside her apartment. I didn't bother to knock. Holding the nearby banister for support, I lifted my knee to my chest and kicked the door in.

It was a one-room flat and the Murphy bed was down. The Krause girl was sprawled on the sheets, moaning and groaning. Ordinarily, I would have rushed over to her and administered mouth-to-mouth resuscitation, except by the look of things, that was exactly what her boyfriend was already doing. He was on top of her and they were going at it like a couple of rabbits in heat. The sound of the stereo must have muffled the crash of the breaking door.

"Excuse me," I said while the moaning got heavier, "is this the Krause residence?"

They stopped in mid-thrust and looked at me. Instinctively, the boyfriend fell off her and they both pulled the sheets up to their necks, staring at me in a mixture of fear and curiosity.

"I'm sorry to interrupt," I said, a little embarrassed. "I know how annoying it can be to have someone interrupt. I usually lock the doors and put the phone off the—"

"Who *are* you for Christ's sake!" the Krause girl demanded, "and what the hell do you want?"

"The name's Slade," I said. "I'm a private dick out of New York City. I wanted to ask you a few questions."

"Ever hear of knocking?" the boyfriend asked. He was a pimply eighteen-year-old with a crew cut and a tattoo of a battleship on his upper arm.

"I would have knocked," I said, "except that when I was coming in a wanted murderer was coming out and I thought you might have needed help."

The boyfriend sighed at that one. Then he got up, keeping the sheet wrapped around his thin body, grabbed his sailor suit, and headed for the john. He knocked my shoulder roughly as he went by. I didn't blame him.

Also sighing, the Krause girl got up and slipped into a robe. She turned the stereo down low and poured herself a glass of bourbon. She didn't offer me one.

"I'll make it short and sweet," I said. "Jack Mushnik is dead and I'm after his killer. I need all the help I can get."

"Jack's dead?" she asked. I nodded. "Poor Jack. He was a really nice guy. He wanted to save me from a life on the streets. I told him I was going home to Indiana, but all I did was change my address and phone number. Poor Jack."

"What can you tell me about Al Greco's?" I asked. "How long have you worked there?"

She shrugged. "Couple of months," she said. "There's nothing else to tell."

"What exactly goes on there?" I asked.

"You gotta be kiddin'," she said. "Whadaya think goes on there? It ain't a day-care center."

"So all you do is give massages to people?"

She rolled her eyes for some reason. "Yeah right," she said. "We give massages to people. People with sore backs and knotted-up muscles."

"How many times did Jack come around?" I asked.

"Just twice. Just to talk to me. Jack never laid a hand on me. He was a gentleman."

"Are you sure?"

"That he was a gentleman?"

"That he just came around twice?"

"Well, I only saw him twice," she said. "But I only work three days a week on account of I'm new. They do most of their business on the weekends."

I wasn't getting anywhere. I had the feeling Gilda Krause was hiding something—it had to do with the way she averted her eyes.

"Look," I said gently, "if there's something you want to tell me, don't be afraid. You won't get in any trouble. I'll see to it personally. Ever hear of immunity?"

"Sure," she said. "It has to do with the production of antibodies and their effect on alien microorganisms."

"That's right," I said. "If you talk I can get you a requisition for a month's supply of Erythromycin from the police."

I could see that she was tempted by my offer, but all she did was shrug and shake her head. "I'd help ya if I could," she said. "But I don't know nuthin'. Sorry."

At that point, her boyfriend, all dressed up in his navy blues, came out of the john and knocked me again as he walked by. This time I wasn't amused, so I grabbed him by the neck flap and shook him.

"Watch it, hot stuff," I said, "or I'll knock your butt from here to the nearest poop deck."

"Tough guy, huh?" he said angrily, pulling loose from my grip. "Mr. Macho."

"You bet, Ace," I said. "I was in the Marines once. Infantry. In the last war. I used to eat guys like you for breakfast."

"Oh, yeah?" the dumb punk said defiantly. "Go ahead. Try it. Here's some salt and pepper. There's ketchup in the fridge. Mustard too."

"We're out of mustard," Gilda said.

"Push off, punk," I said to the guy. "I ain't in the mood for wiseguys."

He stared at me for a few seconds before shoving off. As soon as he was gone the

Krause girl warmed up to me. I could tell she liked her men rough and tough.

"You're pretty tough, aren't ya?" she asked, putting a hand on my knee.

"I get around on my fists all right," I said.

"That sounds like a pretty clumsy way to get around," she said. "Ordinary walking would be faster."

She was starting to come on strong, so I backed off and headed for the door. "I gotta go," I said. "Watch yourself, okay? And if you get any sudden insights, here's where you can reach me."

"Okay," she said. "Sure you don't wanna stay for a drink?"

"Some other time," I said. "But thanks."

❑

If Moose Lebowitz hadn't come to pay a call on the Krause dame, where had he been? I took the stairs two at a time until I was in the entrance vestibule again. I checked all the names on the mailboxes until I found the one I was looking for—a Mrs. Clyde G. Griswald on the fourth floor. It must have been pure coincidence that the former owner of Al Greco's lived in the same apartment building as the Krause girl.

I knocked this time and a boozed-out, bleached-out, wrinkled dame of about sixty or so opened the door as far as it would go with the chain latch still on and peered at me through the space.

"Mrs. Griswald?" I asked.

"Yeah?" she said suspiciously. "What do *you* want?"

"The name's Slade," I said. "I'm a private detective. Could I come in and ask you a few questions? It won't take long."

She closed the door, undid the latch, and let me in. The place was a mess. Empty booze bottles were everywhere. The bed was unmade and there was a swamp growing in the sink.

The Griswald dame retired to a beat-up old armchair, poured the last few drops of booze into a dirty glass, and moved the hem of her stained robe farther down over her knee. If she was afraid I was going to make a pass at her, she had nothing to worry about.

"What's on your mind, good lookin'?" she asked.

I settled into a chair opposite her. "Did you have a visitor earlier this morning? A big guy about six eleven?"

"Sorry, pallie," she said, "I didn't hear you."

I took my rum flask out of my breast pocket and poured a few drops into her glass. She sipped it. "Good stuff," she said. "Now, what was that you said?"

"Did you have a visitor earlier this morning?" I repeated. "A big guy around six eleven?"

"It wasn't at six eleven," she said. "It was closer to 9:30."

"I was referring to his height," I said.

"You mean Moose," she said. "Yeah, he was here. Is he in trouble already?"

"Yeah," I said. "Lots of trouble. What did he want?"

"He wanted to know where Peaches was," she said. "She used to work for my late husband, may he rest in peace. Best stripper in town. I told him that poor Peaches had died about nine or ten years ago."

"Anything else?" I asked.

She extended her glass and I refilled it. "Wanted to know where she was buried. I told him Forest Lawn, not too far from the grave of my Clyde, may he rest in peace. Mob did him in about the same time Peaches bit the big one. Poor Clyde."

"Did he say where he was going?"

"No, but I figured he was going to heaven. Clyde was always a good man."

"Moose," I corrected.

"Nope," she said, "but wherever it was, he was in an awful hurry to get there. Didn't so much as say a good-bye. Just tore out of here like he was late for an appointment."

I got up to leave. "Thanks," I said. "Mind if I use your telephone?"

She wavered for a second, but when I poured the last drops out of my flask for her, she nodded toward the phone.

I dialed Lieutenant Tennant's number. "It's Slade," I said. "Your pal Lebowitz was in the vicinity of Elmhurst and Western about ten minutes ago, driving a white Caddie, and heading north on Hollywood Boulevard. You owe me one, Lou."

I hung up and looked over at the Griswald dame to thank her again. But she was sound asleep, snoring through her wart-ridden nose, the dirty booze cup dangling from her index finger by its handle. Not wanting to wake her, I tiptoed toward the door and let myself out.

Though Gilda Krause had tried her best to come off as the picture of innocence, I had the gnawing feeling she was hiding something. Jack wouldn't have gone to all the trouble of his little Hollywood charade if there wasn't something sinister lurking behind the thin red curtains at Al Greco's House of Massage. And whatever it was, the Krause girl was obviously too scared to spill it to the likes of me. It could have been anything—drugs, blackmail, white slavery—and I knew that sooner or later I'd have to find out the truth.

In the meantime, though, I had suspects

to question. Marty Kahn, the agent, was at the top of my list, so I found a pay phone not far from the Krause girl's apartment and called his office to set up an appointment. A dame with a British accent answered the phone and put me on hold for over ten minutes, standard procedure in Hollywood if you're not a big fish.

"I'm sorry," she said when finally she'd gotten back on the line. "Mr. Kahn is taking a meeting. Any message?"

"I'll call back later," I said and hung up. I knew if I left a message, it'd be weeks before he got back to me. Agents are like that.

I grabbed a bite to eat at a nearby greasy spoon, topped it off with a can of beer, and headed out to Rita Klondyke's place in Bel Air. I knew from the movies that she was a doll with a figure that could cause a man's drool to start flowing like whitewater rapids. I knew a few facts too, mostly stuff I'd picked up from the gossip rags. It was the typical Hollywood success story—she'd come from a poor German immigrant family named Schmutz, been discovered by a small-time talent agent in a chorus line in New York, shipped out to Hollywood for the standard studio screen test, gotten a few minor roles, slept her way up the studio ladder, and wound up a star, complete with name change, phony bio, and an entourage of press agents, publicity flacks, and managers. Like most Hollywood star types, she'd been through four marriages, mostly guys she'd dumped once they couldn't do anything more for her, had a few kids scattered around the country, gone through the usual drug rehabilitation, and was rolling in dough. Of course, rolling in dough wasn't enough to make her happy—I'd learned that on a Barbara Walters special.

I parked my heap between a Rolls-Royce and a Bentley on a pleasant tree-lined street in Bel Air and knocked on Rita Klondyke's massive front door.

A Chinese houseboy answered the knock, all smiles.

"The name's Slade," I said. "Mac Slade, private dick. Is the missus in?"

"You the third detective today," he said, beaming for no ostensible reason. "Last one much plettier. Much plettier!"

He made a whistling sound and licked his lips. I figured it couldn't have been Tennant—he was cute, maybe, but hardly pretty. No, it had to be Quinn. Damn her for getting there before me.

The Chinese houseboy led me down a

long garden path, past a huge kidney-shaped pool, through a cabana, past a Jacuzzi, past another pool, this one pancreas-shaped, to a small wooden structure about the size of a two-car garage. At the door, the houseboy knocked, announced me, waited for a positive response, then ushered me in and shut the door behind me.

It was dark and smoky inside and incredibly hot, and it didn't take me long to realize I was standing in the middle of a sauna bath. Once my eyes had adjusted to the darkness, I spotted the Klondyke dame sitting on a bench clad only in a skimpy white towel, sipping on a Bloody Mary. The sight of her gorgeous body made my tongue fall out of my mouth, but I rammed it back in with my fingers and lodged it behind my front teeth so it would stay put. Beside her, also wrapped in a towel, was an older guy with a pukka-shell necklace dangling over tufts of damp chest hair and an ill-fitting toupee resting uncertainly on his noggin.

"I've been expecting you, Mr. Slade," the Klondyke dame said in that unmistakable voice I'd heard cooing in countless movies. "Ms. Quinn said you'd be around sooner or later."

That one bugged the hell out of me, but I swallowed it for the time being.

"This is Murray Pester, my press agent," she continued. I shook the guy's hand and sat down on one of the benches. It must have been over 120 degrees in that room and I could practically feel my shoes sweating.

"I won't take up much of your time," I said. "I just have a few questions."

"Miss Klondyke will do her best to accommodate you, my friend," the press agent said. "She recognizes this interview as part of her civic duty and—"

"That's swell," I said, interrupting the blowhard. The Klondyke dame gave me a hidden smile. "Now, Miss Klondyke," I said, deliberately ignoring Pester, "how well did you know Jack Mushnik?"

"Not very well," the press agent said. "She'd seen him at a few of Armando's parties, bumped into him several times at restaurants. They were nothing more than casual acquaintances."

"I didn't ask you, pal," I said. "I asked Miss Klondyke."

"And Miss Klondyke answered you," he said with an edge to his voice. "Through me."

"I get it," I said. "She's the ventriloquist and you're the dummy. Is that it?"

I thought I caught a tiny giggle emanating from Rita Klondyke's lips, but I could have been mistaken. Pester shot me a look that could have welded two pieces of cast iron together.

"If you've got another question, please ask it," he said curtly. "Miss Klondyke's time and mine are valuable."

"Anybody mind if I take my shirt off?" I asked. "It's gotta be 120 in here."

"It's 122 to be exact," the press agent said.

"Now who was that talking?" I asked. "You or Miss Klondyke? I'm just curious."

Pester didn't answer. Shrugging, I removed my jacket, which by now felt like it had just come out of the rinse cycle, and then peeled off my shirt, which had stuck to my skin. I saw the Klondyke dame's face light up when she caught her first look at my physique.

She turned to her press agent. "Listen, Murray," she said pleasantly, "I appreciate your coming around today to help, but I think I can handle Mr. Slade myself. He looks pretty harmless to me."

"That's okay, sweetheart," he said. "I

think I'll stick around. That's what I get paid for."

The star gave him a strained smile. "Good-bye, Murray," she said firmly. "I *said* I think I can handle Mr. Slade myself."

Pester finally got the message. He stood up, wrapped his towel tighter around his waist, and headed for the door. "Ciao, baby," he said to his client. "I'll be at the studio later this afternoon. Call me."

"See ya around, pest," I said.

"Pest*er*," he corrected me, and with that he was gone.

Once the door had bolted shut, Rita Klondyke looked at me and smiled. "Sorry about that, Mr. Slade," she said. "Murray does try a little too hard sometimes, but he means well. And he does manage to keep the press out of my hair most of the time."

"If you don't mind," I said, "I'd like to get back to my questions. I've got a lot of calls to make today and it's hotter than hell in here."

She got up, brushed by me, and turned the heat down. Within a few seconds, the steam cleared and for the first time, I got a good look at her, that million-dollar body clad only in a terry-cloth towel. When she was done with the heater, she came over and sat down next to me. I could feel her eyes on my body.

"Where did you get muscles like these?" she asked.

"There was a sale at Sears," I said. "I picked up the set for just under fifty bucks."

I wanted to continue questioning her, but she'd put her long slender hand on my right bicep and I could feel my blood racing. Before I knew it, she was looking into my eyes and I felt like I was in one of her movie love scenes.

"You know what I think, Mr. Slade?" she murmured, caressing my shoulder muscles. "I think that beneath those cold, steely blue eyes of yours beats the heart of a truly sensitive man."

"Your anatomy's a little off, baby," I said. "My ticker ain't located in my head."

She smiled weakly. My response hadn't been in her script. "You think you're pretty tough, don't you?" she said.

"I don't think," I replied.

"I'd noticed that," she said. "Would you like to feel *my* muscles?"

I must've been nuts to turn down an offer like that, but I had business to do and the time clock was running down. "I would *like* to finish this interview," I said firmly. "Now be a good girl and let me do my work, okay?"

She pouted for a second like most dames do when yours truly gives them the brush-off, but then a smile came back to her face and she took her hand off my body. "Shoot," she said.

I figured I'd start in with a general question that didn't refer to Jack's murder but nonetheless tested her memory for details. That was my standard ploy—if the details were right in one area and wrong in the other, I had a lead.

"Tell me what you did the day of Jack's murder," I began.

"That's an easy one," she said. "I got up around six o'clock, jogged for an hour, worked out in my gym for an hour, took a Jacuzzi and a sauna, had my hair done, went for a manicure, saw my therapist, then my chiropractor, had my usual vegetarian lunch, swam in the pool for an hour, took another Jacuzzi, talked to my agent, had a facial and a massage, then went to Armando's party."

"Sounds like an intellectually stimulating day," I said. I'd been taking notes while she'd talked and now I was ready to spring the big question. "Let's hear your alibi," I said.

She sighed. "I wasn't even at the party when Jack was killed," she said. "I'd left early. I was tired. I'd had a rigorous day and I wanted to get a good night's sleep. I got home around eleven o'clock. My houseboy, Lo Fat, fixed me a nightcap and I went to bed."

"A nightcap?" I asked. "What kind of nightcap?"

"A vodka gimlet," she said.

"Have you got any idea at all why Jack was killed and who would want to see him dead?" I asked.

She shook her head. "None," she said. "No one knew him that well. He was just a hanger-on, somebody who tagged along to get a little shine from the edge of the spotlight. There are lots of people like Jack in Hollywood."

"How well do you know Marty Kahn?" I asked.

"Pretty well," she said. "He's my agent."

"Would Kahn have any reason to want Jack dead?"

"I doubt it. Marty's a shark—that's why he's my agent — but his bark is worse than his bite."

"Shark's don't bark," I said, sensing a discrepancy in her story. "What about this Elvira Swann dame? She have any reason to want Jack out of the way?"

"Not that I'd know of," she said.

I folded up my pad and stuck my pencil in my jacket. I was done for the time being. Noting that the interview was over, the Klondyke dame started playing with the hair on the nape of my neck. In a matter of seconds, her other hand was rubbing my thigh. My blood started to boil.

"Want to feel my muscles now?" she said.

I couldn't stop what was happening even if I'd wanted to. I took her in my arms and her lips found mine in the warm darkness as if she'd always known where they were, an inch below my nose. With her hands roving madly around my half-naked body, her tongue explored my mouth as if she was trying to see if I still had my wisdom teeth. Madly, passionately, she tried to devour me.

"Oh, Mac," she moaned. "It's been so long since I've been with a real man."

While we caressed, I could hardly believe what was happening. There I was, being made love to by the most desirable matinee idol in America, the dame that wet dreams are made of. And there I was, a moment or two later, pushing her away, peeling her smooth arms off my body, prying her wet lips off mine with my fingers. I must've been nuts, but I knew I couldn't let myself get involved with a suspect. Not until I got my revenge on Jack's murderer.

She looked disappointed as hell when I stood up and put my sopping shirt back on. "What are you doing?" she asked, nonplussed. "You're not giving me the cold shoulder are you, Mac?"

"At this temperature, it's more like the hot shoulder," I said. She was pouting, so I lifted her chin and gave her a peck on the lips.

"It's no good, baby," I said. "I'm a dick and I'm afraid you're still a suspect. I'd love to jump in the sack with you, I'd be crazy not to, but I can't. You understand, don't you?"

"I'm used to getting what I want, Mac," she said. "You're the first man who ever turned me down. What kind of stuff are you made of?"

"The usual," I said. "Membranes, corpuscles, enzymes, organs, ectoplasm, gray matter, bile, ducts, veins, arteries. . . ."

"What about hormones?" she asked.

"I got hormones all right," I said. "But they're not on active duty at the moment."

I made for the door. "Call me sometime, Mac," she said. "If you change your mind."

"You got it, baby," I said. I took one last look at her, swallowed the lump that had formed in my throat, and went out into the cool air.

❑

I reentered the Klondyke dame's house and looked around for the houseboy, Lo Fat. If anyone could corroborate her alibi, he could. After meandering through about ten rooms and five hallways, I found him in one of several dens reading a copy of *Variety*.

"Keeping up with the Hollywood gossip?" I asked him.

"No sir, Missa Srade," he said. "I writing movie sclipt. Many car chases! Beautifur gills! Lotsa sex and viorence too! You wanna read?"

"I'll pass," I said. In Hollywood, everybody was writing a script. Even houseboys. That's common knowledge.

"The night Miss Klondyke came home from Armando's party," I said. "Do you remember about what time that was?"

He thought for a second. "Sure do, Missa Srade," he said. "About ereven o'crock. I just get back from walking dogs. Arways walk dogs about ten-thirty."

"And you fixed her a nightcap, right?" I asked.

"That's collect," he said. "I fix Miss Krondyke a blandy. Collect."

"Are you sure it was a brandy?" I asked. "Are you sure it wasn't a vodka tonic or a bourbon and soda?"

"Arways fix blandy," he said. "Not good at mixing drinks."

So, I'd caught Rita Klondyke in her first lie. She'd said Lo Fat had fixed her a vodka gimlet; he insisted it was a brandy. Granted, it was a minor point, but she'd managed to remember all the other minor details of her day, why the discrepancy over something as easy to recall as a nightcap?

"Mind if I use the phone?" I asked the houseboy, who'd gone back to scanning the glossy pages of *Variety*.

"Phone in den," he said, pointing down the corridor. "First door on light."

I thanked him and made my way down the hallway. First, I dialed Marty Kahn's office again. The same English dame answered the phone, put me on hold for ten minutes, then told me that Marty was on long distance to New York. This time I left a message and gave my motel number.

Next, I called Tennant's office.

"Did you nab the big guy?" I asked when his secretary put him on the line.

"Dammit, no!" he said, sounding a little frustrated. "I put out an APB on the car and about an hour later a couple of cruising patrolmen spotted it parked in front of a hotel called the Palm Palace in East Los Angeles. Moose was registered there but he must have taken a powder."

"How do you know?" I asked.

"We searched the hotel from top to bottom. All the talcum had been stolen."

"That's odd," I said. "What's your next step?"

"Beat's me," he said. "Guess we'll just have to wait, stay on the lookout."

"I'll let you know if I spot him," I said. "I seem to run into him a lot these days."

"Get anything on the Mushnik murder yet?" he asked.

"Nothing much," I said. "The Klondyke dame's story seems to add up, except for a few little details. I haven't been able to get a hold of Kahn yet."

"Neither have I," Tennant said. "That's

Hollywood for you. Who's next on your list?"

"Elvira Swann, the psychic," I said. "She oughta be good for a laugh or two."

"Call me if you get anything," he said.

I told him I would, hung up the phone, and made for my heap.

Elvira Swann's house was in Brentwood, and by the time I got to the Sunset overpass of the San Diego Freeway I could feel the cool ocean breezes through the open side vent of my car. The clean air felt good but it didn't do much to clear out my brain, which was already getting a little fogged by the contradictory details of this case. So far, I had nothing much to go on. Aside from the nightcap discrepancy in Rita Klondyke's alibi and the fact that Quinn had gotten back to town a little too fast for my money, I didn't have the slightest inkling as to motive. Who would have wanted Jack out of the way—and why? Had someone penetrated his guise of Hollywood hanger-on and discovered that he was a detective? Was he on to some deep, dark secret that revolved around the massage parlor? Obviously, someone was hiding something and until I found out what that something was, I knew I'd just be going around in circles.

The Swann dame's place was a small two-story affair, set back off the street, shaded by a couple of oversize walnut trees. It looked like something out of a Norman Rockwell sketch, a New England–style home with bay windows and an enclosed front porch, white clapboard walls, and a shingled roof. The door knocker was a brass replica of a horned Satan complete with talons and spear. I decided to knock with my fist instead.

The door opened immediately, as if I'd been watched from the inside, and the lady of the house poked her face through the door crack. For some reason, I'd expected Elvira Swann to be a crotchety old gypsy in colorful robes and lots of cheap costume jewelry—after all, she was a fortune-teller. But she wasn't anything like that: She was around thirty, had one of those perfect faces that looked like Michelangelo had sculpted it, and, when she opened the door, I saw that she had a body to match the kisser—slim and small-breasted, but firm and muscular.

"Mr. Slade," she said in a breathy, mysterious voice, "we've been expecting you."

"How'd you know who I was?" I asked, as I walked into the foyer.

"There is very little that I don't know, Mr. Slade," she said, moving about the room like some kind of inebriated gnome, her white robe billowing around her gorgeous legs. "Actually, Ms. Quinn said you'd be around sooner or later."

I swallowed hard on that one, but didn't say anything. She was leading me into a room that was separated from the foyer by a beaded curtain. The walls were decorated with enlarged replicas of tarot cards, and staring at me from a cage suspended from the ceiling was a large black bird that looked like Howard Cosell.

She motioned for me to sit down opposite her at a table upon which rested a large crystal ball. "I know exactly why you're here, Mr. Slade," she said in that weird, gaspy voice. "You wish to know my alibi and to ask me about the murder of Jack Mushnik. So far you have no clues at all, no motive, nothing. I am afraid that I will not be able to help you much. While the murder took place I was reading the palm of the agent Martin Kahn. Armando was at my side the entire time. Miss Klondyke, who you also suspect, had departed an hour or so earlier. Give me your palm."

While she'd been talking, yours truly had been unable to take his eyes off the V of her low-cut gown. It was made of a sheer fabric that fell an iota short of showing the complete picture of what lay beneath it. Absently, I gave her my palm.

She examined it, tracing the lines. "Hmmm," she said.

"What do you see?" I asked.

"A great deal of sweat," she said. "Also, your life line and your love line intersect in precisely the same way that the San Diego Freeway and the Santa Monica Freeway converge. There is one crucial difference, however."

"What's that?" I asked.

"Your palm lacks an off ramp."

I sighed and withdrew my palm. "Cut the baloney, lady," I said. "I don't buy that stuff."

"I've taken the liberty of doing a chart on you," she said, getting up and taking a stack of papers off a bureau. She swished back to the table like a deranged nymph.

"It's a very interesting chart indeed, Mr.

Slade," she said. "It shows Uranus in ascension."

I grabbed the papers from her, half expecting to see a picture of me with my naked butt in the air, but all I saw were a bunch of lines that looked like a weather chart.

"As you'll note," she said, pointing to the chart, "there's also a cold front coming in from Canada that ought to hit a high pressure system later this week."

I tossed the charts on the floor. "Look, lady," I said, "I don't go in for any of this hocus-pocus. If you're such a big cheese in the fortune-telling racket, why don't you just stroke your crystal ball a few times and tell me who murdered Jack Mushnik."

"That's an easy one," she said, brushing a speck of dust off her shoulder. "It was J. C. Quinn."

❑

Her accusation stopped me cold in my tracks. I was struck speechless for half a minute or so and just peered into those cold gray eyes of hers to see if they could tell me if she was on the level or not. But they told me nothing and just stared back like a pair of lifeless agate marbles.

"How can you say that?" I asked finally.

"By the movement of my tongue against the inside of my mouth," she said. "Otherwise known as speech."

"I mean where do you get the idea?"

She shrugged. "Haven't you ever heard of the Process of Elimination?"

"Sure," I said. "I use the process of elimination every morning on the can. But what I want to know is what gives you the idea that Quinn is the guilty party?"

"As I said before, Armando, Kahn, and Klondyke all have solid alibis. That leaves Quinn. Where was she when the murder was committed? Admit it, Slade—the thought has crossed your mind too."

I nodded. "But what's the motive?" I asked. "Quinn had no reason to kill Jack."

"How do you know?" she asked. "Perhaps Jack had found something out about Quinn and was preparing to spring it on her. You're the detective. You figure it out."

I had to admit, charlatan that she was, the Swann dame had succeeded pretty well in reading my mind. The more alibis I heard, the more I suspected Quinn. She was certainly strong enough to have lifted Jack into the fridge and smart enough to have pulled off an undetectable murder. Undetectable if yours truly hadn't chanced by at exactly the wrong time. I wanted to ask Elvira Swann a few more questions, but we were suddenly interrupted by the clang of her phone.

Instead of answering it, she let it ring twice and said to me, "It's for you."

I was skeptical, but I picked up the receiver. Much to my surprise, she was right—it was Tennant.

"Meet me at Forest Lawn as soon as you can get there," he said all excited.

"What for?" I asked.

"You wouldn't believe me if I told you," he said. "Come see for yourself."

Before I had a chance to say anything more, he hung up. I put the receiver back in its cradle. The Swann dame was staring at me with those steel-gray eyes of hers, no doubt trying to look into my mind to see what I was thinking. I decided to use the opportunity to rattle her a little.

"Gotta go," I said, grabbing my hat.

"What's the rush?" she asked. "I'm rather enjoying this little tête-à-tête. Stay, have a drink, ask me some more questions."

"Can't," I said. "That was Lieutenant Lou Tennant of the LAPD. Seems he's chanced upon a major breakthrough in the case. Which way do I go to get to Forest Lawn?"

My little fib had done the trick—it had rattled her. She didn't say anything for a good thirty seconds, just stared off into the distance. I waved my hand in front of her to get her attention back to earth.

"Hey," I said. "Forest Lawn. Which direction?"

"East," she said absently, as if part of her mind was still exploring the stratosphere. "Go east on the Ventura Freeway and follow the signs."

"Is something wrong?" I asked.

That got her back down to earth. "No," she said abruptly. "Nothing's wrong. What should be wrong?"

I thanked her for her time and patience, gave her limp hand a perfunctory shake, and let myself out.

❑

The freeway was empty so I put the rental heap on overdrive and cruised along, all the while turning over in my mind Elvira Swann's eerie reaction to my little spiel about a breakthrough in the investigation. Something had certainly shaken her up, and I knew instinctively that I had blundered into my best lead so far. I still didn't have a motive for Jack's murder, but I had a pretty solid hunch that Swann and her gang were involved somehow. Maybe their alibis were all solid, but this was Hollywood and alibis can be written and rehearsed just like a movie script.

Police cars lined the gate in front of Forest Lawn, so I parked behind Tennant's heap and walked in the direction of the shining flashlights. On the way, I stopped to read a few of the tombstones. One said, "Here Lies Sol Binsky, Producer. He Gave Good Meeting." Another quipped, "Marvin Stein. Forever in Turnaround." The place gave me the willies.

Tennant was standing in front of an open grave, peering into it with a flashlight. Beside him was an empty coffin. Next to that was a shovel. At the head of the grave a couple of detectives were questioning a black man, no doubt the cemetery's night watchman. He had a nosebleed and was wiping the blood with a dirty rag.

"What gives?" I asked, standing next to Tennant and peering down into the empty grave.

"About two hours ago, the night watchman was making his rounds," Tennant said. "He spotted a big guy digging up one of the graves. He ordered him to halt.

The big guy socked him in the nose and knocked him unconscious."

"So what?" I said. "Sounds like an ordinary case of grave robbing."

"I don't think so," Tennant said. "Look at this."

He pointed the flashlight at the empty grave's head, illuminating the tombstone that had apparently fallen over. The words carved into it gave me a chill. They said: "Peaches Moskowitz 1954–1974."

"Lebowitz," I said.

Tennant nodded and turned to one of his men. "Where's that spade?" he asked.

"I's raht heah, Lieutenant, suh!" the black night watchman said.

"Not *you,*" Tennant barked. "The *shovel.*"

One of the detectives handed him the shovel. Tennant took it by the digging end and shined the light on the handle. It was muddy and you could see the print of a huge thumb etched clearly into the dried mud like a fossil formation.

"Hardly any point in checking for prints," Tennant said. "I'm certain it was Moose. The crazy bastard dug up her corpse and went off with it. Probably stuck it in the trunk of his car."

"What's your angle?" I asked.

"It seems obvious," Tennant said. "The crazy s.o.b. is obsessed with this Peaches Moskowitz. God only knows what he plans to do with her body."

"Maybe he's planning to have her stuffed," I guessed. "Or maybe—"

"Don't say it," Tennant interrupted. "Some things even a homicide detective can't stomach."

I closed my yap and stared down into the empty grave. A fog was settling over the landscape and the place looked like something out of a B horror film. It was very quiet for a few minutes. Tennant sighed wearily and was about to head back to the cars, when the police radio started to crackle.

Within seconds, a uniformed cop ran up to Tennant. "Homicide, Lieutenant," he said, out of breath. "Just came over the radio. Beverly Hills." He had the information written down on a piece of paper, which he handed to Tennant.

"Oh, Christ," Tennant said, crumpling the paper in his hand. "This is Marty Kahn's address."

❑

Tennant put his siren on and, with me tailgating him in my rental heap, we made it to Beverly Hills in record time. Standing outside Kahn's huge colonial mansion was a large woman, who identified herself as Kahn's German housemaid, Greta Hassenpfeffer.

"Mein Gott!" she said, all aflutter. "Vun moment, he's shvimmen in de vasser, und da next moment he's shvimmen in yellow . . ."

Clearly, the woman was beside herself and therefore not making any sense. Tears overcame her and she wept copiously. Tennant calmed her until the tears subsided and gently cajoled her into leading us to the body.

"Zis vay, *mein Herren,*" she said, leading us out to the pool. We stood there for a moment, staring in disbelief at the sight of Marty Kahn, frozen in the center of the pool, his arms outstretched in a dive formation.

"Yust like I said," Greta continued. "Shvimmen in yellow."

Tennant and I ventured closer to the pool and soon it was all clear. The surface of the water shimmered with what the maid had called "yellow." She'd meant Jell-O. Marty Kahn's body was frozen in a poolful of hardened green Jell-O. I stuck my finger in and sampled some.

"Mmm," I said. "Lime. My favorite."

Tennant glared at me. "Jesus, Slade," he said. "There's a dead man in there. Have a little taste, will ya?"

"I just *had* a little taste," I said.

While Tennant and his men dusted for fingerprints and checked the pool equipment, I took Greta Hassenpfeffer aside and asked her a few questions. Between sobs, she was fairly cooperative. She told me that Kahn had come home around five thirty, taken a shower, had a drink, spent twenty minutes in the Jacuzzi, and eaten a salad.

"Then what?" I asked.

"Zen, zat detective fraulein vas here und asked Herr Kahn some qvestions," she said.

"Detective fraulein?" I asked.

"Ja, ja," Greta continued. "Such a nice girl. Blond hair, blue ice. Aryan."

The description fitted Quinn to a tee. So she'd gotten to Kahn while everyone else had failed. I wondered how she'd done it.

"When did she leave?" I asked.

The maid thought about it for a moment. "Maybe vun hour ago," she said. "Maybe two."

"And where were you when Mr. Kahn took his little swim?"

This angered her. "*Ich*?" she bellowed.

"I vas doing my duty in za house, of course! I was following Herr Kahn's orters! I saw nussink!"

"Now, now," I said, trying to calm her down. "Don't get yourself into a furor."

Her eyes bulged out at this one. "Vat does za Fuehrer haff to do vis zis?!"

I sighed and left her to her work. Tennant was standing by the poolhouse, lost in thought.

"Look at this," he said, pointing to a huge bag labelled "chlorine powder." I stuck my hand in the sack and removed a sample of the light green powder.

"Taste it," Tennant ordered.

I looked at him to see if he was serious. He was, so I placed a few bits of the stuff on my tongue.

"Hmmm," I said when the powder's tang hit my taste buds. "I didn't know they made flavored chlorine. What will they think of next?"

"It's not flavored chlorine, it's lime Jell-O mix," Tennant said. "Somebody must have made a substitution."

"Any theories?" I asked.

"I'm not sure, but I think I've figured it out," he said. "Tell me how this sounds: The murderer substitutes Jell-O powder for chlorine. Since it's lime, it doesn't show in the dark. The poolman, or someone impersonating the poolman, comes and dumps a few pounds of the stuff in the pool. Kahn comes home at five-thirty this P.M. and turns the pool heater on, thus cooking the Jell-O. He then goes into the house for an hour or so to wait for the pool to heat up. He comes out, turns off the heater, and gets on the diving board. The night chill causes the Jell-O to harden instantly, Kahn dives, and he's trapped. What do you think? You think the theory gels?"

"It gels all right—it was the perfect crime. No suspect in the vicinity, no murder weapon, no fingerprints," I said. "By the way, the Kraut dame told me that Quinn was here an hour or two ago."

"That's interesting," Tennant said. "You think she did it?"

"I don't know," I said, walking Tennant to his car. "What can you tell me about Kahn? Any dirt on the guy?"

"Plenty," he said. "For starters, he had a prison record."

That one took me by surprise. "Are you saying that Kahn was a con?" I asked.

"That's right," Tennant said. "I had some of my boys look into his record. He spent a few months in the cooler back in 1978."

"I'll be damned," I said. "What was the rap?"

"Real estate fraud," Tennant said. "The usual shady land deal."

"What kind of shady land deal?" I asked.

"It was your basic fraud case," Tennant said. "Kahn started out a realtor. He'd sold a house to a couple of newlyweds. They'd wanted a place that got full sun all day, but Kahn sold them a place with a shade tree on the property. Just your typical shady land deal, like I said."

"That doesn't help me much," I said.

Tennant got into his car and I closed the door for him. He rolled down his window. "Do me a favor," he said. "Keep an eye on Quinn for me. I've got my hands full as it is."

I nodded and stood on the curb, watching as Tennant put his buggy in gear and disappeared around the corner.

Marty Kahn's bizarre murder threw a monkey wrench into the case because it opened up a whole slew of new possibilities. Had Kahn been murdered because he'd known who'd killed Jack? Had Jack's murderer croaked Kahn to keep him quiet? Had my little charade about a breakthrough in the case caused the Swann dame to alert the murderer? Or had Quinn gotten the goods on Kahn and taken her revenge on him? A thousand questions entered my poor cluttered mind, but not a single concrete answer exited. If I was going around in circles before, now I was doing pirhouettes and figure eights.

One thing I knew for sure—the key to this mystery lay hidden somewhere at Al Greco's House of Massage. Jack had gone there to find a runaway and had stumbled upon something big, something that he wasn't supposed to know about. If I could find out what that something was, I'd be able to start putting the pieces of the jigsaw together. I knew the cops had searched the place after the manager had been murdered, but I also knew that they probably hadn't done a very thorough job of it. After all, the murder had been fairly cut and dried, and once I'd identified Moose Lebowitz as the suspect there'd been no real reason for Tennant's men to give the place a total going-over. So, even though it had gotten late and I was dead tired, I decided to head over to Al Greco's and see if the coppers had overlooked anything.

I parked about fifty yards down the street from the massage parlor and walked the rest of the way. The cops had sealed off the place, due to the murder, so I snuck around to the rear of the building until I found a window big enough to accommodate my size. The window had been padlocked from the outside and taped on the inside in the usual fashion. Having picked my share of police padlocks, I was in the building in a matter of seconds.

It was pitch dark in the joint, so I switched on my pocket flashlight and started looking around. First, I rifled through all the desk and file drawers in the manager's office, then I went from massage cubicle to massage cubicle thoroughly going over every possible drawer and closet. Next, I felt along the walls and floors for hollow areas and, finally, I let my fingers explore the base of every lamp and light fixture in the joint. I even unscrewed every on/off switch, checked behind mirrors and wallhangings, and looked for stitch marks in the mattresses. All in all, it took about an hour to go over every inch of the place but, much to my surprise, I didn't find a damn thing. Yet somehow, I knew there was something there. There had to be. I could feel it in my bones.

I only had two rooms left to search—the bathrooms. But I had a sinking feeling that I wouldn't find anything in either of them—bathrooms were too obvious and only the rankest of amateurs hid things there. Besides that, sticking my hand down a toilet bowl was hardly my favorite pastime.

I started with the men's room, which was cleverly labeled "Playboys." It looked like it hadn't been cleaned since the McCarthy era—there were bacteria hardening on the toilet bowl that hadn't been identified yet by modern science. Nonetheless, I stuck my hand down the toilet bowl, looked under the tank lid, took apart the urinal, tapped all the pipes, glanced under the sink, felt behind the mirror, and pulled the paper towel dispenser off its bearings. But just as I'd figured, there was nothing there.

With my filthy hands propped up in front of me like a surgeon entering the operating room, I made my way to the ladies can, which, natch, was labeled "Playgirls." This one, at least, was semi-clean, and I went through the exact same ritual all over again. Unfortunately, I came up with the exact same result—*nada.*

I stood there in the center of the room for about five minutes trying to figure out what, if anything, I'd overlooked. As far as I could tell, I'd covered every nook and cranny. Only two possibilities remained—either there was nothing to be found or someone had been here before me and cleaned the place out.

Before exiting the joint, I went over to the dames' sink to wash my hands. I'm no health nut, but I figured there was enough bacteria on my hands to get a good epidemic of black plague going, so I banged the powdered soap dispenser with the heel of my palm and emptied out enough cleanser to get a nice, foamy lather going. Only there was one problem—no matter how much soap I used or how hard I rubbed, I couldn't get a lather up. In fact, the powder felt more like sandpaper than soap.

It dawned on me in a flash. I pulled the soap dispenser off its screws, dried off my hands, and put a little sample of the powder on my tongue. The numbness started immediately. It was cocaine. At least a pound of it. Street value about twenty grand, maybe more.

Just to make sure, I took about thirty or forty snorts, then a couple more for the road, until I was sure it was cocaine. Only cocaine would make me feel like I felt at that moment—like running from here to Sacramento and back. So that's what Jack had been onto—Al Greco's was nothing more than a front for a coke dealership. Old Jack must have blundered into it—maybe he'd mistakenly gone into the ladies' room or maybe he'd seen a transaction being made behind one of the thin red curtains. Maybe he'd even searched the manager's office and found a client list. Judging from Jack's guise as a Hollywood hanger-on, the clientele must have been quite a star-studded crowd.

Finally, it was all starting to make sense, all of it except for one minor detail: I still didn't know who had killed Jack.

❑

Needless to say, I wasn't able to get any shut-eye that night, not until I'd walked around the block 417 times and belted down at least ten jiggers of rye in my motel room. By four in the morning I was finally out, and when I woke up the next morning I had a hangover that was complicated by one of the worst cases of sore feet I'd ever experienced. On top of that, my nostrils felt like somebody had cleaned them out with an electric drill.

It was a warm breezy morning and still early, so I decided to head on over to Quinn's place unannounced. I wanted to see what she was up to, keep an eye on her for Tennant like I'd promised, spec out her digs, and generally take her by surprise. I also wanted to find out if she'd gotten anything worthwhile on Marty Kahn.

Quinn had a condo in the Wilshire district, a few blocks east of Rodeo Drive. It was in one of those modern four-story buildings with floor-to-ceiling windows, a pool, its very own health club, sauna, Jacuzzis, the works. The rent must have been at least a thou a month, if not more. I pulled up into the circular drive and let a red-coated valet park my heap.

A security guy in the downstairs lobby used a house phone to inform Quinn that she had a visitor. After what seemed like a moment of hesitation, he waved me in. I grabbed an elevator to the fourth floor, walked down a lushly carpeted hallway, and knocked on Quinn's door. Darkness shrouded the peephole and five seconds later the door popped open.

She was wearing a pair of tight jogging shorts over a red leotard that was stretched tautly over her ample breasts, pushing them together like a pair of mating blowfish. I must have interrupted her in the middle of her morning workout because she was breathing hard, an action that caused her gorgeous orbs to rise up and down as if a midget were inside her shirt blowing up balloons. She was some dish, all right, but she didn't seem too thrilled to see me. As a matter of fact, she was glaring.

"Mind if I come in?" I asked, breaking the silence.

She hesitated for a moment or two, contemplating her options, then nodded begrudgingly and ushered me in without a word of greeting. I figured she was still nursing a grudge over our last little tête-à-tête in Jack's office. After locking up, she turned that taut body of hers toward me, planted her hands on her hips, and watched me as I wandered casually around the room, examining art objects and fondling the fabric of her furniture.

"Nice place you got here," I said, picking up a Waterford vase. "Very nice. Maybe even a little *too* nice for a private dick."

She didn't say anything, but I could tell she was angry. Sighing, she walked into the kitchen to pour herself a cup of coffee. She didn't offer me one.

I sat down on the couch. "What's the matter, Quinn?" I asked. "Cat got your tongue?"

"That's right, Slade," she said. "The same cat that dragged you in. The same cat that curiosity killed."

I laughed. She was a tough cookie all right. My kind of dame—tough, beautiful, and quick with the repartee.

"Aw, come on, Quinn," I said in a mock-serious tone. "Give a guy a break, will ya? If it's an apology you want, you got it. You can't nurse a grudge forever. You can send it flowers and a get-well card, wish it a speedy recovery, and hook it up to an I.V., but sooner or later you gotta stop nursing it."

I glanced over at her to see if my little speech was thawing her out, and thought I caught a glimmer of hope, an almost imperceptible twinkle in her gorgeous blue eyes. On the other hand, maybe it was just my imagination.

"Look, Quinn," I said, "I won't mince words. I won't puree or mash them either. We've both got the same goal—to get the son of a bitch who murdered Jack. Sure, you and I got off to a rocky start. But let's let bygones be bygones. After all, bygones aren't good for much else, and just maybe, if we put our heads together, we'll be able to put a few more pieces into the jigsaw puzzle."

"Nice speech, Slade, real heartrending," she said, "but I'm onto your little game. You didn't get to Kahn and I did and you want to know if I learned anything."

"You got me there, sweetheart," I said, "but I got a few things up my sleeve besides just my arm."

"Like what?"

"Like what Jack found at Al Greco's," I

said. "What got Jack into this mess in the first place."

That news stopped her in her tracks. "You're bluffing," she said.

Without a word, I reached into my breast pocket and took out a little square packet made of toilet paper. I handed it to her.

"This is what Jack found at Al Greco's?" she said. "Toilet paper?"

"Open it up," I said.

She peeled the leaves back until she came to the matted powder inside. Like a pro, she wet her index finger, dipped it into the stuff, and gave it a taste.

"Snow," she said.

"It's not *snow,*" I said wearily. "It's cocaine. Pure stuff. I found about a pound of it hidden in the joint last night. There was probably more, but I wouldn't be surprised if someone cleaned the place out before I got there. Al Greco's is a front for a coke smuggling ring with a list of clients that'd blow this town wide open. And Jack was out to infiltrate their organization. He got too close and somebody bumped him off. Still think I'm bluffing?"

She shook her head and handed the packet back to me. But she didn't say anything.

"Well, what's it gonna be?" I asked impatiently. "Do we play ball or what?"

"Okay, you win, Slade," she said. "I did a little research on Al Greco's myself. A friend of mine over at the County Records Bureau looked the place up in the files. Al Greco's House of Massage is owned by a dummy company named Paramount Enterprises. Paramount Enterprises is owned by none other than our friend Marty Kahn."

"Nice work," I said. "So you think Kahn killed Jack?"

"There's more," she said. "Kahn's silent partner is Rita Klondyke."

"That fits," I said, putting two and two together. "Kahn killed Jack because he knew too much about Al Greco's and Rita Klondyke killed Kahn because she didn't want to be implicated."

"Possibly," she said tentatively. "Apparently, Klondyke and Kahn had a vicious argument at Armando's party. Kahn was her agent and she threatened to leave him because he hadn't gotten her any meaty roles lately."

"Who'd you get that from?" I asked, impressed by the extent of her research.

"Armando," she told me. "But there's something fishy about all this. It all fits a little too snugly. It's all a little too pat. Too rehearsed. Too . . . Hollywood."

I sat back and lit a cigarette. "Okay, I'll concede that the Klondyke business sounds a little shaky, but Kahn sure sounds to me like he had a hell of a motive for murdering Jack. Jack was onto his drug sideline and there was a lot of money at stake."

"Okay," she said. "That washes. But who killed Kahn?"

I took a deep drag of my Camel. "Who hated him enough to kill him?" I asked.

"Are you kidding?" she said. "He was an agent. Everybody hated him."

"What about his clients?"

"Especially his clients."

"I don't get it," I said.

"You have to understand what makes this place tick," she said, educating me in a gentle, noncondescending way. "Hollywood is a funny place and it's not anything like other towns. Nothing is really as it appears to be here. The town is built on pretense and images. Everyone is the writer, director, and special effects technician of their own lives. You can't believe anything you hear or see. It's all façade. Pure make-believe. Get the picture?"

I nodded. "Thanks for the crash course,"

I said, "but you still haven't told me what you got out of Kahn or how you even managed to get in to see him."

"Easy," she said. "Kahn had a notorious soft spot for cute bimbo types, so I put on a tight dress and did a lot of billing and cooing. I let him paw me for awhile, then I identified myself. I even acted like I knew he was the murderer. I came on real strong, even pulled a gun on him. I told him the jig was up and he'd better spill his guts."

"And did he?"

"Yeah," she said. "He spilled his guts all right. All over this new sweater I'd just gotten at Magnin's. The dry cleaner said it had a fifty-fifty chance of pulling through."

"That's tough," I said.

"Comes with the territory," she said, settling back on the sofa. "It would have been worth it if I'd gotten something out of him, but I didn't."

I drew another cigarette out of my pack and lit it with Quinn's coffee-table lighter, one of those gift shop gizmos that look just like a revolver. After I'd taken a few contemplative drags, Quinn sighed, got up, and went into the kitchen. I followed her and leaned against the fridge as she made us both a drink.

"I hear you've been helping Tennant with the Lebowitz case," she said. "Very charitable of you. Tennant needs all the help he can get. His heart's in the right place, but his brain isn't."

"I'll drink to that," I said, taking a long sip of bourbon. "How do you know Tennant?"

"I've known him for years," she said. "We interned together at the D.A.'s office our senior year at UCLA. Put together the file on Lebowitz as a matter of fact."

"He didn't tell me that," I said.

"I'm not surprised," she said. "We dated for awhile. He asked me to marry him. He wanted a housewife type, but I wanted a career, so I turned him down. He's had it in for me ever since."

"He's got you on his list as a suspect in the Mushnik murder, you know," I said.

She laughed. "That figures. Lou Tennant would like nothing more than to grill me under the hot lights of the precinct station. I get a lot of parking tickets too." She took a short sip of her drink. "Am I on *your* suspect list too?" she asked.

"Mine?" I said, feigning surprise. "Not a chance!"

She looked into my eyes. "I doubt you're telling the truth, Slade," she said, "but it doesn't matter. You'll see the light sooner or later."

She was standing awfully close to me at this point and I could smell the perfume wafting off her gorgeous bod. I put my drink down on the kitchen counter and let my hand slip around her slender waist. When she didn't resist, I pulled her close to me and drew her lips to mine. But as we kissed, I saw her left hand open the refrigerator and reach into the freezer. Then she pulled away from my embrace and handed me a package of meat—it was a shoulder of pork. I got the message right away—she was giving me the cold shoulder.

"Sorry, Slade," she said. "I'm still a suspect remember? Dicks and suspects don't mix."

"Too bad," I said. "You and I could make beautiful music together, baby."

"I doubt it," she said. "I'm tone deaf and, besides, my ukelele needs new strings."

I looked into her eyes and knew from her expression that she was on the level. Sighing, I emptied the rest of my drink and headed for the door. On the way, with my back toward her, I lit another cigarette with her coffee-table lighter and then surreptitiously stuck the revolver-shaped gizmo into my jacket pocket. The fingerprints on it would reveal whether or not she really was a suspect and I wanted that issue cleared up before the next time we saw each other. Then I made for the door.

"So long, Slade," she said. "Better luck next time."

I was angry and confused by the time I'd left Quinn's building and walked down the circular drive in search of the valet. Angry because someone had gotten to Jack's killer before I could exact my revenge; angry because I was going to be deprived of the pleasure of watching a little weasel like Kahn grovel for his life at my feet; and confused because neither Quinn nor I had a decent lead concerning Kahn's murder, other than the very thin thread linking Rita Klondyke to the case.

The valet took about twenty minutes to find my rental heap, then had the unmitigated nerve to ask for a tip. I told him "Seabiscuit in the third at Santa Anita," and tore off down the drive and onto the street.

I needed some quiet time to think things out, so I drove around for awhile, down palm-lined streets, past pink and white stucco houses, along LA's wide boulevards and bright, muraled building walls, past the garish billboards that lined Sunset and the mortuary ads on every bus-stop bench. If Marty Kahn had indeed murdered Jack, as all logic said he did, then technically my job was done—I was free and clear to go back to New York with no strings on my conscience. Yet I knew I couldn't leave. The case intrigued me too much. My instinctive curiosity compelled me to keep on digging.

While the landscape sped past me in a blur of color, I tried to piece the elements of the case together, fitting each of my four suspects into the scenario. Assuming that Kahn had killed Jack because Jack was onto his drug ring, who had knocked Kahn off and why?

First on my list was the Klondyke dame—her partnership in the massage parlor business gave her the most obvious motive. As a major star, she had the most to lose if Kahn implicated her in Jack's murder. Also, as Quinn pointed out, she had threatened to sever her client relationship with Kahn the night of Armando's party. Had Kahn blackmailed her, had he threatened to implicate her if she left his agency? Or, had she feared that Kahn was on the verge of being caught by the coppers and that he would be better off silenced? Attractive as those motives were, there was something just a little too obvious about them.

Next on my suspect hit parade was Elvira Swann. As far as I knew, she had no motive whatsoever, but I continued to be haunted by her nervous reaction to my little charade about a police breakthrough. Though I doubted that she had murdered Kahn herself, I had a solid hunch that she had alerted the guilty party—after all, Kahn had been croaked while Tennant and I were looking for clues at Forest Lawn. She'd been the only one to know that I'd be out of circulation for that crucial hour or two. Had she alerted the Klondyke dame? Had the Klondyke dame gotten scared and bumped off Kahn? Or had someone else been alerted?

The only two remaining possibilities were Armando and Quinn herself. So far, neither Quinn nor I had been able to get a single shred of evidence linking Armando to anything in this case. His alibis all checked out and he seemed clean as a whistle. That could mean one of two things—either he was innocent or he was just better at covering his tracks than any of the others.

And last but far from least, there was Quinn herself. Try as I might, I couldn't stop suspecting her. The same hypothetical scenario kept popping into my mind—Jack finds out that Quinn's linked to Marty Kahn's drug operation; onto Jack's investigation, she goes on vacation, comes back a little early to nail Jack, trumps up some evidence linking Jack's murder to Marty Kahn, then bumps off Kahn. It was more of a hunch than anything, but I was still bothered by the obvious luxury of Quinn's apartment and her speedy return to town following Jack's murder.

As luck would have it, my destinationless journey had taken me to Beverly Hills, and I found myself driving down the palm-lined street that Armando lived on. Though it was nothing more than pure coincidence, I decided that as long as I was in the neighborhood I'd drop in on the little pansy and see if I could get any dirt out of him. It was still early in the day and I'd have plenty of time to regrill the Klondyke dame later on in the afternoon.

I drove right up to Armando's front door and rang his chimes. Twenty seconds later, the door swung open and, framed in the doorway with a look of utter surprise on her finely chiseled features, was none other than Elvira Swann. I knew that she and Armando were pals, so I shouldn't have been surprised to see her in his house, but the fact that she was wearing a bathrobe and a towel turban on her head as if she'd just exited hastily from the shower, gave me pause.

"Well, well, well," she said after she'd caught her breath. "If it isn't Mr. Slade. What a surprise!"

"Surprise?" I asked. "I didn't know psychics could be surprised."

"Yes, well, won't you come in?" she asked nervously, fidgeting with the buttons on her robe. I entered the house and shut the door behind me.

"And while we're on the subject," I said. "You were wrong about the weather too."

"The weather?" she asked hesitantly.

"The cold front from Canada, remember?"

"Ah, the cold front!" she said. "Yes, well,

you win a few, you lose a few. Shall I see if I can find Armando? It *is* Armando you came to see, isn't it?"

"That's amazing!" I said sardonically. "You figured that out all by yourself? You *are* psychic!"

She laughed nervously, her smile clearly strained. "I'll see if he's around," she said. "I just came over to use the shower. My hot water heater's on the fritz."

With that, she swished down the hallway and disappeared around a corner. I heard her voice lilting, "Armando! Oh Armando! Where are you, dear? You have a caller," followed by Armando responding, "I'll be there in a minute, sweetie."

It was a lot more than a minute, closer to twenty. I was leafing through a colorful coffee-table magazine on interior design when Armando pranced in waving an empty cigarette holder and acting ever-so-happy to see me. He was wearing a plaid smoking jacket and purple ascot—very stylish—and he smelled like somebody had dipped him in a vat of eau de cologne.

"Why, Mr. Slade!" he exclaimed. "I can't tell you how positively sublime it is to see you."

"Then don't," I said.

He smiled out of the corner of his mouth

and put a butt into his cigarette holder. After flicking nothing but sparks out of his coffee-table lighter, he slammed it back down on the table, and, sighing, I handed him Quinn's revolver-shaped gizmo. He looked at it for a moment.

"And what, pray tell, is *this?*" he asked.

"It's a lighter," I said. "Just pull the trigger."

"Amazing!" he said, turning it over in his lily-white hands. "It looks just like a gun."

"Brilliant deduction," I said.

Shrugging, he found the trigger and put his index finger on it. "Like this?" he asked. I nodded wearily. Shrugging again, he pulled the trigger. A shot rang out and I felt a bullet whiz by my head and slam into a Chinese vase, smashing it to smithereens.

"Sorry," I said after I'd recovered from the shock. "I must've mixed them up in my pocket. Here's the lighter."

I grabbed my trusty roscoe out of his hands and handed him Quinn's lighter. He wasn't too thrilled about the vase, but he didn't say anything about it, just lit his cigarette and leaned back on the couch, blowing smoke rings.

"So, Mr. Slade," he said, "what brings you around here? Surely you don't suspect little old me of any wrongdoing?"

"I didn't know that you and the Swann dame were so cozy," I said.

"We're friends," he said, "and that's all. She wanted to use my shower. That's not against the law, is it?"

"Is she still around?" I asked.

"No, I'm afraid she's left," he said. "Important luncheon engagement, I think she said. In Malibu."

"That's funny," I said. "How come I didn't see her leave?"

"Back door," he told me. "I imagine your presence in the front of the house scared her off."

"I see," I said. "Are you implying she's got something to hide?"

"Don't be silly, Mr. Slade," he chortled. "It's just that you're always suspecting people. That's your business, I realize that, but it tends to make one a little nervous in your presence. Do you mind if I call you Mac?"

"Yes," I said.

That stiffened him a bit. He sat upright, crushed out his butt, and gave me the phoniest smile I've seen in years. "All right, *Mr. Slade*," he said in a very businesslike tone. "Ask me what you came to ask me and make it snappy. I'm a busy man you know."

"I assume you've got an alibi for the

night Marty Kahn was murdered?" I asked.

"As a matter of fact," he said, "I happened to have been with Ms. Swann that evening. She was doing my chart. You can check it out with her if you like."

I shook my head. "Funny how everybody's always having their charts done or their palms read everytime somebody gets knocked off around here."

"I don't see the humor in it myself," he said seriously, "but if you say it's funny, I'll be happy to laugh." He stood up, rubbed out the wrinkles in his smoking jacket, and strode over to the other side of the room to pick up the pieces of the shattered vase. Somehow, I'd gotten on his bad side and he was trying to make it plain that the interrogation was over. I watched him for a second and then popped the Big One.

"Did Marty Kahn supply you with drugs?" I asked.

That startled him. He craned his neck and stared into my eyes, trying to figure out how much I knew. "Maybe he did and maybe he didn't," he said. "In any case, I'm not a big user. Strictly small potatoes."

"Did you know that Jack was onto the Kahn/Klondyke drug ring?" I asked.

"Of course not. I never even knew Jack

was looking into it. And even if I had, I wouldn't have cared. Frankly, I've never cared much for Marty, and I strongly doubt whether Rita even knew about Marty's little sideline."

"What makes you say that?" I asked.

He shrugged. "Marty's been investing his clients' capital for years," he said. "People like Rita Klondyke have so much money, they tend not to keep track. Besides, with all her wealth, why would Rita even need the small change Marty made on his sordid little drug enterprise?"

"But if Rita had found out, what do you suppose she would have done about it?" I asked.

He shrugged. "She probably would have scratched him to death with her fingernails," he said casually. "I absolutely adore Rita, but she's got a bit of a temper and she's very protective of her reputation. Ask anyone."

I had the feeling he was telling the truth—after all, I'd experienced Rita Klondyke's temper myself and I'd met her press agent.

Armando, meanwhile, was making a big show out of looking at his watch, so I stood up.

"I don't mean to be rude," he said,

meaning just that, "but I've got a very important appointment and I'm already terribly late."

I made for the exit. "No problem," I said, slapping on my fedora and swinging the front door open.

"*Ciao,*" Armando said, giving me a little wave as I headed for my car. "And next time, Mr. Slade, do me a favor."

"What's that?"

"Bring a book of matches."

❑

Since the Swann dame was out to lunch, I figured I'd kill off the afternoon reinterrogating Rita Klondyke. What I needed to find out from her was where she'd been when Kahn was murdered and whether or not she knew anything about the agent's shady drug dealings. After driving around Beverly Hills for fifteen minutes, I spotted a pay phone behind a Bob's Big Boy on Robertson and called the Klondyke house.

Her houseboy, Lo Fat, answered the ring and said his boss was at the studio and wouldn't be home until 2:30. I told him to tell her I'd come around then and, with another two and a half hours to kill, I decided to pay a call on Lieutenant Tennant at headquarters.

I found him with his feet propped up on

his desk, studying a manila folder full of papers. He looked even more fatigued than he had the last time I saw him.

"Make any headway?" I asked.

He nodded and tossed the manila folder across his desk. "Take a look at these," he said.

I shuffled through the folder, which was crammed with pieces of light blue stationery, all covered with a nearly indecipherable handwriting.

"What are they?" I asked.

"Letters," Tennant told me. "Love letters. We found them in Kahn's bedroom the other night."

I looked at them again. They all started out with "Dearest M." and closed with "Your eternal Lover, E."

"They're from that Swann woman," Tennant said. "Pretty hot stuff. I've been scanning them all morning for clues and now I feel like I could use a cold shower."

"I didn't know they were an item," I said.

"Neither did I," Tennant mused. "Take a look at the postscript on the last letter in the bunch."

I read it aloud, stopping whenever the chicken scrawl got too hard to decipher. "P.S.," I read, "Dearest, please try to forget what I told you in a moment of weakness last night. I know A. doesn't trust me and suspects that I told you. Whatever you do, don't let on to A. that you know UNDER ANY CIRCUMSTANCES."

"What does it mean?" I asked, putting the letter back in the folder.

Tennant shrugged. "It probably doesn't mean squat," he said. "The letter *A* could stand for Armando, but he's a hairdresser and most likely is privy to lots of gossip. I imagine Armando passed on some gossip to Swann, Swann passed it along to Kahn, and then got worried that Armando would find out. The capital letters made me think it might be something serious though. There's an urgency to it. But offhand, I'd be inclined to rule Swann out as Kahn's murderer. The last letter is dated three days ago and it's just as hot as the rest of them."

"Hmmmm," I mused, trying to digest the news and come to some kind of logical conclusion. "I'm thinking out loud here, but maybe, just maybe, jealousy figures in here as a motive for Kahn's murder."

Tennant furrowed his brow. "What are you getting at?" he asked.

"I'm not sure," I said, "but according to Quinn's research, Rita Klondyke was pretty ticked off at Kahn for some reason, even threatened to find another agent. Maybe there was more between those two than just business. Maybe she was in love with him, found out about the Swann dame, and killed him in a fit of jealous rage."

Tennant shook his head. "If it was a fit of jealous rage," he said, "she would have stabbed him or shot him, but she certainly wouldn't have gone through all the aggravation of hardening him in a poolful of lime Jell-O. It doesn't wash."

"I'm not so sure," I said. "Rita Klondyke is used to getting what she wants. Plus she's as calculating as a dame can get. You don't make it as far as she's gotten in show business without being a calculating woman."

Tennant shrugged. "Maybe," he said, "but I can't get a conviction on the basis of that. I need evidence, Slade. Solid evidence."

"I'm working on it," I said. "In the meantime, I think I know who killed Jack Mushnik."

He bolted forward at his desk. "Who?" he asked, his eyes alive for the first time in days.

"Don't get too excited," I said. "The finger of guilt appears to be pointing at Marty Kahn. I'm 90 percent sure. I snooped around Al Greco's last night—"

"So it was *you!*"

"Right," I said. "I found about a pound of coke in the ladies' john. Our agent friend owned the place and had a lucrative little sideline going. Jack was onto his operation and the rest is history."

"That adds up," he said. "We found a few vials and a client list in Kahn's house. Pretty star-studded crowd too. If Jack was really onto them, his investigation could have blown the lid off this town. You think maybe Kahn was done in by some big shot on the list trying to keep his rep clean?"

"Could be," I said, taking Quinn's revolver gadget out of my pocket, "but that's a hell of a long list and it would take us months to get to all of them. Half of them are probably out of the country shooting films. So I suggest we stick with what we got so far. And in the meantime"—I handed him the gun lighter—"do me a big favor, will ya? Have the fingerprints on this checked out and run them through the computer for a matchup."

He fondled Quinn's lighter. "Whose is it?" he asked.

"Your pal Quinn's," I told him.

"You think *she* did it?" he asked, eager for me to say yes. "Jesus, I'd give anything to finger Quinn."

"Keep your sexual fantasies to yourself," I said.

"Can you see the newspaper headlines?" he asked, sweeping his hand in the air as if there was a newspaper in front of him. "HOMICIDE LIEUTENANT FINGERS LADY DICK. Wow! I can see the LA *Times* running it in their Metro section."

"More likely, the *National Enquirer* would run it in their Pervert of the Week section," I said. "But don't count your chickens, Lieutenant. It's only a hunch—one out of several. By the way, you didn't tell me you and Quinn went to college together."

"Didn't seem relevant," he replied.

"Probably isn't," I said. "What else do you know about her? Does she come from money?"

He shook his head. "No, Albuquerque," he said.

"I mean, were her folks well off?" I asked.

"Not as far as I know," he said. "Her mother was a widow on a fixed pension. Quinn was on scholarship at UCLA and worked nights at some joint on Sunset. But that was ten years ago. Why?"

"No reason in particular," I said. "Just background." I got up to leave. "Get some shut-eye, Tennant," I ordered, "and let me know as soon as you get anything on those prints."

It was only 1:30 by the time I emerged from the police precinct so, with another hour to kill before my appointment with the Klondyke dame, I decided to do a little snooping around at Elvira Swann's place in Brentwood. Odds are she was still out to lunch—Hollywood lunches can go on for hours—and I needed the time to find out if she was hoarding her own cache of love letters from Kahn. If so, the answers I still needed might be hidden there.

I parked about two hundred yards past the Swann dame's house and backtracked through her neighbor's well-tended garden until I arrived at the psychic's back door. Just to make sure, I knocked a half dozen times, and when I was satisfied that no one was around, I stuck a credit card into the crack of the flimsy screen door and, with one expert flick of the wrist, flung the latch out of its receptacle.

The back of the joint was a mess—stacks of old astrological charts and manila dossiers littered an old rolltop desk that faced the back garden. I rifled through every drawer, through the piles of old tarot cards, through old texts on phrenology, astrology, alchemy, palmistry, through stacks of client bar graphs, even through a stack of tax returns from 1974 to the present.

As I was searching, I must have knocked the tax returns off the desk because one near the bottom—for fiscal 1976—fell open on the floor. Something in it caught my eye and I picked it up and leafed through it. Stuck in the middle of it, in a pile of loose receipts, was a check stub made out to Elvira Swann. The balance was $15,000 and the payer was none other than Jack's landlord, Armando Eclair.

Why would Armando be writing checks to the Swann dame for $15,000? Was it a loan? Had she been blackmailing him? I stared at the stub but it revealed nothing.

Flipping through the rest of the 1976 tax return I learned only one thing that didn't seem relevant—Elvira Swann had moved to Los Angeles in 1976 from Milwaukee, Wisconsin. Her income in the Midwest had been practically nil, but after her first year in Tinseltown, she'd managed to make an adjusted gross income of $35,000, not including the check from Armando. I was impressed. In fiscal 1976 my adjusted gross income wasn't even worth adjusting.

The rest of the tax returns revealed nothing, and since I hadn't located any love letters in the back room, I moved on into the parlor where the Swann dame conducted her little psychic tête-à-têtes. Careful not to disrupt anything, I searched the drawers and cabinets, found nothing, then moved on to her bedroom.

The room was sparsely laid out, with only a large canopied bed against one wall, a drawerless dressing table against the opposite wall, and a large double-doored armoire to the right of the bed. Sighing, I went for the armoire first, figuring that if a dame like Swann had love letters, she'd probably either keep them with her valuables or in an old purse stashed away behind the furs.

There was something stashed away in

that armoire all right, but it wasn't an old purse with love letters in it.

It was the Swann dame herself.

❑

Ordinarily, I love it when dames fall into my arms. Live dames anyway. Dead dames is another story. And the Swann dame was definitely dead. The second I swung the armoire doors open, she collapsed onto me and, not knowing right away that she'd bitten the Big One, I caught her. Then I looked at her—her eyes were bulging out of their sockets, her body was limp, and her throat had a set of black and blue thumbprints that I recognized immediately They were the same thumbprints I'd seen on the muddied shovel at Forest Lawn just a few days before. Elvira Swann's strangulation was the handiwork of none other than Moose Lebowitz.

I stood there for about thirty seconds, holding up the Swann dame's limp body, then dragged her to the bed and laid her out. Tough as I am, the experience had rattled me and I sat down, lit a cigarette, and waited for the blood to return to my face and for my hands to stop trembling. I've seen dead bodies before, plenty of times; I've tripped over them, accidentally sat on them, even used them for doorstops, but this was the first time one had actually fallen on my head. If nothing else, it was a new experience, one that I hoped never to repeat.

All the while, I tried to figure out why Moose Lebowitz had killed her. It just didn't add up. It had also never occurred to me that the two cases were in any way connected. What did a depraved mug like Lebowitz have to do with this high-rolling Hollywood gang? Moose's sole motivation, from what I'd been led to believe, involved exacting his revenge on the Peaches Moskowitz dame, the stripper who'd set him up ten years before. Not only was it seemingly cut and dried, he'd already swiped the Moskowitz dame's corpse from its grave in Forest Lawn. So why this senseless murder?

Once I'd gotten a grip on myself, I phoned Tennant and gave him the facts. He sounded just as perplexed by it as I was. Within twenty minutes of placing the call I heard the police sirens wailing down the street, and ten seconds later Tennant and a few of his flunkies appeared in the Swann dame's bedroom.

I crushed out my cigarette while Tennant ordered his men to photograph the corpse and dust for fingerprints.

"Was it laid out on the bed like this?" he asked me.

"Nope," I said. "It was propped up in the armoire. Ever play a round of medicine ball with a cadaver?"

He shook his head. "What makes you think Moose did it?" he asked.

"Take a gander at the thumbprints on her neck."

He took out a magnifying glass and examined the corpse's Adam's apple. "Those are Moose's prints all right," he said. "I don't get it. It doesn't make any sense. You think it's just a coincidence?"

"I don't know what to think," I said. "All I know for sure is a lot of strange things have been happening ever since that Lebowitz mug came to town. Five'll get you ten he's involved in this whole sordid mess somehow."

"But how?"

"Beat's hell out of me," I said. "I never figured him into it, neither of us did. A couple of things bother me though."

"I'm all ears," Tennant said.

"You know you're right," I said, noticing the size of his lobes for the first time. "You ought to let your hair grow longer on the sides, cover them up a little."

"I mean, I'm *listening,*" he said.

"Yes, well, what bothers me is this: number one, I bumped into the Swann dame not more than an hour and a half ago at Armando's. Supposedly she was hurrying off to a lunch date in Malibu. Now, you know as well as I do that Hollywood lunches go on for hours. How could she have been here getting herself killed and at lunch in Malibu at the same time?"

"Maybe she cancelled and came home," Tennant mused. "What's number two?"

"Number two is a bowel movement. Everybody knows that," I said wearily.

"I mean, what's number two on your list," he said. "You said two things bothered you and number one was the Swann dame's lunch engagement."

"Oh yeah," I said. "Number two is this: Before I found the body, I happened to come across the Swann dame's tax returns. I don't know what it means, but in 1976 Armando gave her $15,000, enough to set her up in this house as a psychic and freelance charlatan."

Tennant stroked the blond stubble on his chin. "They're friends," he said. "We've already established that. Maybe she needed some financial help. Maybe it was just a loan between friends. I'll admit it's interesting, but what does it lead to?"

I shrugged, glanced down at my watch, and slapped on my fedora. It was 2:45. Time to play footsy with Rita Klondyke.

"Did you get a readout on those prints I asked you to check yet?" I asked Tennant as I headed for the door.

"I'd just fed them in when you called," he said. "I ought to have them in about half an hour."

"Good," I said. "I'll be at the Klondyke dame's place. Let me know what you find. I have a feeling, just a feeling, mind you, that we're very close to solving this thing."

"What gives you that idea?" he asked.

"Simple," I said. "There's only one chapter left after this one."

❑

Before driving over to Rita Klondyke's place, I used Tennant's phone to call Quinn. My cover story was to see if she'd made any headway in the case, but actually I wanted to keep tabs on her whereabouts. If my interview with Rita Klondyke pointed the guilty finger at Quinn, I wanted to know where she'd be. After three rings, her answering service picked up and told me that she could be reached at another number. The number was Armando Eclair's private line.

I climbed into my rental buggy and tooled out to Bel Air. It wasn't until I'd gotten to the third or fourth stoplight that I was sure I was being tailed. I tried to slow down enough to get a peek at who was following me, but whoever it was knew enough to keep two or three cars behind me at all times. All I managed to get was a good look at the car—it was a blue '79 Ford—and I figured it was just one of Tennant's flunkies keeping an eye on me. I didn't mind at all—frankly, if I was going to be tangling with a murderer within the next few hours, a police tail might even come in handy.

I pulled up to the Klondyke house about twenty minutes later and Lo Fat let me in. As he led me through the maze of rooms and out to the garden, I spotted a guy in a pair of Bermuda shorts taking another path toward the mansion's front entrance. He was a young guy, handsome and muscular, a body-builder type carrying a briefcase and wearing a Hawaiian shirt. He seemed to be in a hurry.

Lo Fat led me to a secluded area behind a semi-circle of well-manicured cypresses, and through the steam of the Jacuzzi that was sunk into a redwood deck in the center of the enclave, I spotted Rita Klondyke. She was shoulder deep in the bubbling water and through the vapor clouds I could see that she was in her birthday suit. Lo Fat shuffled off, bowing, and I sat down on a redwood bench, trying to keep from drowning in my own drool.

"Hello, Mac," she said in a low breathy voice that was more of a come-on than a simple amenity. "I've been expecting you for days. What took you so long?"

For a second, the sight of her gorgeous body refracted in the pale blue water caused my larynx to temporarily go on the fritz. I opened my mouth but no words came out. I was momentarily paralyzed by lust. She smiled at me as if she knew the details of every filthy thought that was coursing through my mind.

"I hate to say this, baby," I said after I'd found my voice, "but this ain't a social call. I've got some pretty incriminating questions to ask you and I want some honest answers."

Undaunted by my words, she let her body languish and spread her arms around the lip of the fiberglass pool. "Are you trying to tell me I'm in trouble?" she asked.

"Worse than that, baby," I said. "You're up to your neck in hot water."

"Obviously," she said. "But am I in trouble?"

"Could be," I said, "unless you come up with some pretty convincing answers. For starters, who was the pretty boy I saw leave here as I was coming in?"

"That was Arthur Gonad, my lawyer," she said. "He was just showing me his briefs."

"I'll bet he was," I said. "Why was he in such a hurry?"

"Arthur's always in a hurry," she said.

I took off my fedora and wiped my brow with my jacket sleeve. The heat from the hot tub was starting to get to me. The sight of Rita Klondyke's naked torso wasn't exactly cooling me off either, but I had a lot of questions that still needed answers.

I decided to go right for the tough ones. "The night of Jack's murder," I said, "you claim you came home around eleven o'clock and had a nightcap. You said it was a vodka gimlet but your houseboy says it was a brandy."

She shot me a look laden with guilt. "I lied," she said.

"Mind telling me why?"

"Because I knew that any discrepancy in

my alibi would lure you back here again. And I wanted you back here again to finish what we started last time. If you catch my drift."

I caught her drift all right, but the depth of her calculating mind worried me.

"Why did you threaten to fire Marty Kahn as your agent?" I asked her.

"The usual reason," she said. "He hadn't been getting me any decent roles. And the roles he'd been getting me were few and far between. Last year I only made one lousy film—I played an extraterrestrial nasal specialist in a picture called *Alien Mucus*."

"What about your business partnership with Kahn?" I asked. "Did you threaten to sever that relationship too?"

"You're damn right I did," she said. "When I'd decided to get another agent, I looked into some of the investments Marty had made for me. They included a massage parlor called Al Fresco's or something . . ."

"Al Greco's," I corrected her.

"The last thing a person like me needs is that kind of publicity," she said.

"Did you know that Kahn was using the joint as a front for a cocaine dealing operation?" I asked.

I saw the look of shock register on her face. Clearly, she hadn't known. Faces don't lie.

"That lousy son of a bitch!" she said. "I'd strangle the creep if he wasn't already dead!"

I gave her a couple of minutes to let her anger subside before proceeding with the interview.

"Did you know that Kahn and the Swann dame were seeing each other romantically?" I asked her.

"I'd heard the gossip," she said. "But frankly, I didn't care. Marty's love life was his business."

"How did Armando feel about it?"

"I'm not sure," she said. "Armando and Elvira were pretty close. They'd been friends from way back when. I know Armando never cared much for Marty. I think he thought of himself as being Elvira's protector in a way. It was Armando who actually talked me into dumping Marty as my agent. He didn't think Marty could be trusted."

I sighed. I was getting lots of information, but none of it was leading me anywhere.

"What do you know about Armando?" I asked. "When did you first meet him?"

She thought for a second. "I'm not sure," she said. "He seemed to spring out of nowhere. I first had him do my hair about eight or nine years ago. He came highly recommended by a friend of mine, a stylist. I think he's originally from the Midwest, Cleveland or Milwaukee, I'm not sure."

"And when did you start seeing Elvira Swann?"

"I think it was about the same time I first went to Armando," she said. "In fact, he recommended her to me."

"Interesting," I said, mulling it over. "Interesting but totally useless."

"Do you think Armando killed Marty?" she asked me.

I shrugged. "I doubt it," I said. "The motive's too weak. Just because he disapproved of Kahn's relationship with the Swann dame isn't enough reason for him to commit murder."

As I sat there mulling things over, Rita Klondyke pulled herself out of the hot tub and began to dry herself off. She was doing it in a way that was designed to put my salivary glands into high gear again. When I couldn't take it any longer, I grabbed the end of the towel and tugged her into my arms. As my hands roamed the soft expanse of her naked back, I could feel her knees go limp at my touch. As our lips met, I could hear a soft moan emanate from the center of her being, a moan that turned to a whimper as my mouth devoured hers hungrily. There was an electricity between us, an electricity intense enough to jumpstart a fleet of used cars with enough left over to power a small desk lamp for at least twenty-four hours.

"Oh Mac, oh darling," she moaned, digging her lips into the ticklish part of my neck. "Every molecule in my body is calling out for you."

"I know, baby, I know," I whispered, letting my hands roam madly to her thighs. "And every molecule in my body is waving back."

Our lips had just met again when we both suddenly became conscious of a third voice coming from the edge of the redwood deck. Behind a curtain of Jacuzzi steam was Lo Fat, holding a cordless telephone in his small delicate hands.

"'Scuse prease," he said. "Velly solly to interrupt. Terephone call for Missa Srade. So solly."

Shrugging apologetically at the Klondyke dame, I grabbed the receiver. It was Tennant.

"This better be good, Lieutenant," I said.

"Oh, it's good, all right," he said. "You'll love this. Remember that lighter you gave me, the one with Quinn's prints on it?"

"Yeah?"

"Well, the prints on that lighter match up perfectly to a set of prints that have been in the computer for ten years. In fact, the person belonging to those prints died ten years ago and, until very recently, was buried at Forest Lawn."

The news hit me like a ton of bricks. For a moment or two, I was speechless.

"The prints on that lighter," Tennant said, "belong to Peaches Moskowitz."

I put the receiver back in its cradle and stood there half in shock for a good twenty seconds as the contradictory facts in what had to be my most bizarre case to date began to slowly gel. So it had been Quinn all along, Quinn who had killed Jack, Quinn who had had to silence Kahn, Quinn who had been Moose Lebowitz's girl friend ten years ago. That had been the key—ten years ago. It was then that Peaches Moskowitz, a two-bit stripper at a joint on Sunset, had knocked off a john, implicated Moose, faked her own death, reemerged as J. C. Quinn, gone to UCLA under her new name, and hooked into two partnerships—one with Jack Mushnik and the other with Marty Kahn. Tennant and I had assumed all along that Moose had stolen Peaches' corpse that spooky night at Forest Lawn, but the truth was there'd never *been* a corpse in that grave at all. It had been empty. And just as I'd thought, Quinn had come back early from her so-called vacation, killed Jack, and hurried over to his office to destroy the file on Gilda Krause. Later, when things had started closing in on Kahn, she'd murdered him too to protect her real identity. It had been the perfect setup and she probably would have gotten away with it if yours truly hadn't turned up unexpectedly. Granted, it was bizarre, farfetched and contrived sounding, but what good mystery isn't?

Rita Klondyke had been standing patiently beside me, watching my lips move as I'd pieced together the whole sordid scenario. I didn't have time to explain, so I slapped on my fedora and gave her an affectionate peck on the lips.

"Gotta run, sweetheart," I said, dashing for the front door. "Keep the sheets warm for me."

Before she could even say so much as *"Ciao,"* I was out of the house and galloping for my heap. The blue Ford was parked about fifty yards down the block and I heard its ignition go on as I got into gear and screeched out into the street. Leaning on my horn, I tore down the side-streets, weaving through sluggish traffic like a professional race-car driver, all the time checking my rearview to see if the hound was keeping up. He was.

I screeched to a halt in Armando's circular drive about ten minutes later. As I leaned on the doorbell, I heard the pansy's voice from inside yell, "Keep your shirt on, will ya!" and a few seconds later he'd swung the door open and was standing in the doorway, arms folded, giving me a look that fell somewhat short of extreme annoyance. I didn't care—after all, I was there partly for his own good—and without waiting for an invitation, I stepped gingerly past him into the foyer. Sighing mainly for my benefit, he slammed the door shut.

"Not another round of twenty questions, Mr. Slade," he said, going over to the coffee table. "I'm really not in the mood today."

"Where's Quinn?" I asked.

"She's left," he said. "She was here for

awhile and she left. Maybe half an hour ago?"

"Damn!" I said, socking my fist into the open palm of my other hand. "Mind if I use your phone?"

"Help yourself," he said, settling onto the couch.

I dashed over to the phone and dialed Tennant's number. While it rang, I glanced absently at Armando. He'd taken out his cigarette holder and was about to light a butt. That was when it hit me. If there is one clear moment when all the stray elements in a case come together to make sense, that was it. Suddenly I realized the gaping hole in my theory about Quinn—number one, she didn't smoke, so her fingerprints couldn't have been on the trigger of that lighter. And number two, the person whose fingerprints definitely *were* on the trigger of that lighter was sitting no more than ten feet away from me. It was Armando.

The little pansy must have seen the look on my face change, must have sensed my sudden suspicion, because the next thing I knew he'd pulled a rod out of his pocket.

"What's the big idea?" I asked.

"Don't play dumb, Mr. Slade," he said,

"even though I'm sure it's a role that comes easy to you. Now put the receiver down and move over toward that wall so I can keep an eye on you."

I did like he said, moving slowly so as not to arouse his itchy trigger finger. I could tell it was itchy because he kept scratching it. Besides, he'd killed before, and I didn't want to be the next victim. As he stood up, I wondered what had become of the moron in the blue Ford. With my luck, he'd probably gone out to get a doughnut.

"What have you done with Quinn?" I asked him as he motioned me against the wall.

He smiled menacingly and glanced down at his wristwatch. "By now, your Ms. Quinn is most likely in the final violent throes of a horrible death."

"What have you done this time, Eclair?" I asked, spitting the words at him. "Another death by Jell-O?"

"Something much more horrible, I'm afraid," he said. "Something that would make even *your* blood chill, Mr. Slade."

"Yeah?" I said. "What's that?"

"I've locked your friend Quinn in a room full of Leroy Neiman paintings. She ought to be dead by exposure within . . . oh . . . ten minutes or so."

As the last word left his twisted mouth, I heard a bloodcurdling scream coming from the hallway. It was Quinn going through her awful torture.

"You're a cruel bastard, Eclair," I said.

He shrugged. "I thought I showed a decent amount of clemency in the choice. It was either Neiman or two hours of uninterrupted Wayne Newton tapes through headphones."

The very thought of it made my spine tingle with horror.

"You'll never get away with it, Eclair," I said.

"Very good, Mr. Slade!" he said, clapping his hands together. "That's a very detective thing to say! Very predictable. Unfortunately, I *will* be getting away with it. You see, once you and Ms. Quinn are disposed of, Armando Eclair, poor fellow, will also perish, and a brand new person will spring up in his place."

"Just like Peaches Moskowitz perished ten years ago and Armando Eclair sprung up in *her* place?" I asked.

"Precisely," he said almost proudly.

I shook my head in disbelief. The whole crazy thing was just too bizarre.

"You sure had me fooled," I said. "The mustache must have been what threw me off."

"Does this clear things up for you, Mr. Slade?" he said, ripping off the phony facial hair as if it were nothing more than a Band-Aid strip.

It did more than clear things up—it practically knocked me on my butt. Without the mustache, Armando Eclair was the spitting image of . . . Elvira Swann. That had been the missing key all along!

"I get it now!" I said. "You and Elvira Swann are twin sisters!" He nodded. "So when I knocked on your door unannounced this morning, the person who answered wasn't really Elvira. It was you!"

"Correct," he/she said. "I'm afraid you caught me with my—if you'll excuse the expression—pants down and my mustache off."

As the words spilled out of his mouth, I remembered a few things: how the first time I'd met Armando, I'd thought he would have made a cute dame, and how he and Elvira both had slim, muscular bodies and finely sculpted facial features. But somehow, the depth of their resemblance had eluded me.

"Let me see if I can put the rest of this together," I said as the pieces started to fit in the jigsaw. "Ten years ago, as Peaches, you murdered a guy, set Moose up, faked your own death and burial at Forest Lawn, and reemerged as Armando Eclair."

"Quite right," Armando said. "Poor dumb Moose had a lot of cash stashed away—I needed him out of the way and I needed his money to set myself up in business. I'd always wanted to be a hairdresser, but I lacked the capital to start my own salon. When opportunity knocked, I answered the door, so to speak. Then, of course, I summoned Elvira, told her the whole gruesome story, bought her that little cottage of hers, and set her up in business. Unfortunately, I also felt compelled to do away with Mr. Clyde Griswald, the man who owned the strip joint I worked at. He knew too much. The police concluded that it had been a gangland slaying. I had made it look like that, of course."

"Of course," I said. "And I suppose you killed Jack Mushnik too?"

"I'm afraid I had to," he/she said. "I had nothing against Jack himself. He was a very nice man actually. I liked him in fact. We'd become quite chummy."

"So why'd you kill him?"

"Two reasons," Armando said. "First of all, he was getting a bit too close to finding out about Marty's little drug sideline. I was on the client list and I didn't want the D.A. investigating my past history. But most of all, I killed Jack because I wanted Marty put away."

"I don't get it," I confessed.

"It's really quite simple," Armando said. "Jack was onto Marty's secret drug ring. If Jack was murdered, the cops would inevitably find out about it and point the finger at Marty. And Marty would be sent up the river."

"What did you have against Marty?" I asked.

"Marty was, if you'll excuse the expression, scum. And when he and Elvira became romantically involved, I got very worried and did everything in my power to ruin their little infatuation. After I'd gone to all the trouble of bringing her out here from Milwaukee, set her up in the psychic business, even gave her money to buy that little cottage of hers, she had the unmitigated gall to fall in love with a cheap con artist like Marty Kahn. I just couldn't tolerate it. I knew one day she'd blab it all and that would give Marty the goods to blackmail me. I certainly wasn't about to wait for that to happen. So I set him up before he had the chance to set me up."

"So you killed Jack knowing that the cops would find out about Marty's drug racket and assume he'd been the murderer," I said, my anger rising.

"Very good, Mr. Slade," he said. "I felt Marty had to be nipped in the bud, so to speak. I wanted him put away just like I'd wanted Moose put away ten years ago. But alas, you and that nitwit lieutenant took a little longer to solve the case than I'd expected—and I started to get nervous that Elvira would try to save Marty by telling him all about me and my little ruse. So I had to murder Marty, figuring you and your dumb cop friend would charge Rita with Marty's murder. After all, she was the only one of us with a motive. The one thing I didn't figure on was your exceptional ineptitude."

I ignored this slur. A few details still eluded me and I wanted the answers. "Let me see if I can piece the rest of this together," I said. "For instance, that day I first visited Elvira. I gave her a phony rap about a breakthrough in the case and thought she reacted suspiciously. But it wasn't the breakthrough stuff that had rattled her—it was actually the mention of Forest Lawn that threw her off. So she got scared and alerted you about it. And you figured Kahn had found out about Peaches, so you finished him off with the lime Jell-O."

"Correct again!" he exclaimed. "Poor Elvira did have her moments."

"Is that so?" I said sarcastically. "Then why did you kill her?"

"Oh, I didn't," he said. "I may have had a hand in it, but I certainly didn't do the dirty work. I couldn't kill my own sister, Mr. Slade!"

"Then who did?"

"Why poor dumb Moose did, of course," Armando said gleefully.

I was confused now. "That's what I thought originally," I said. "But why?"

"Simple," he said. "When Elvira figured out that I'd killed Marty, she lost her head and threatened to reveal my true identity to the authorities. Naturally, I couldn't let that happen under any circumstances. But I also lacked the nerve to bump her off myself. So I called Moose in my Peaches voice and asked him to come over and see me. Only I gave him Elvira's address."

That was when I saw the figure dart past the open French doors behind Armando. At first I thought it was my police tail, but when he darted past again, I realized that there hadn't been any police tail at all—the guy in the blue Ford had been Moose Lebowitz. Most likely, he'd been following me from the scene of Elvira's murder in the hopes that I'd lead him to Peaches.

Armando noticed my eyes gazing past him toward the French doors and chuckled. "You can stop the little charade, Mr. Slade," he said. "I'm not going to turn around. There's nothing back there. You'll have to do better than that, I'm afraid."

Meanwhile, Moose had entered the room and was sneaking up behind Armando, his arms stretched out in front of him like a sleepwalker. At the last moment, Armando turned around, having heard Moose's heavy breathing, and a look of pure terror raced across his face. As Moose's hands gripped Armando's throat, Eclair pulled the trigger four times. Even though each bullet found its target, Moose was not stopped. His hands were crushing Armando's throat, and within seconds the gun fell out of the pansy's limp hand.

I pulled my gat out of my pocket,

pointed it in the air to fire a warning shot, and pulled the trigger. I'd been prepared for the shattering blast of the bullet, but all I got was the weak flicker of a flame popping out of the top of the gun barrel. I'd given Tennant my gun and was walking around with Quinn's lighter!

Figuring that there was no stopping a behemoth as determined as Moose, even with the remaining two slugs in Armando's gun, I dashed past him down the hallway in the direction of Quinn's bloodcurdling screams. I knew there wasn't a moment to spare, and if I didn't manage to find her within a few seconds, she'd be a vegetable for the rest of her life.

Racing down the mansion's labyrinthine hallways, I opened every door I came to until suddenly I started to hear the faint saccharine strains of Barry Manilow music emanating from a room in the west wing of the house. So it wasn't just the Neiman torture Eclair had inflicted upon poor Quinn—it was a double whammy—Neiman and Manilow! If anyone could live through that for more than five minutes, it would be a miracle.

Quickly, I dug in my pockets and found a couple of Kleenex tissues, ripped them to shreds, balled them up, and stuck them in my ears. Then, shielding my eyes with my palm to prevent the Neimans from blinding me, I crashed the door in and entered the horrible torture chamber.

I found Quinn strapped to a chair, a gag in her mouth, her eyes taped open. I knew I wouldn't be able to stand it much longer—nausea had overcome me the moment I inadvertently glanced at one of the paintings—so I lifted Quinn's chair into the hallway and slammed the door shut behind me.

Poor Quinn's eyes were glazed over, so I slapped her a few times, removed the gag, and untied her ankles and wrists. She collapsed to the floor, spouting some kind of delirious gibberish.

"Quinn!" I said, propping her head up. "You gonna be all right, kid?"

She didn't respond right away. At first, her eyeballs rolled upward and it looked as if she was going to lose consciousness. But she didn't. Shaking her head to clear the cobwebs out, she started to focus on me. Then she nodded slightly, and I knew she was going to make it.

"I'll be right back," I said. "Don't go away." And with that, I wandered back through the maze of hallways toward the front of the house.

Unfortunately, I was too late to do anything for Armando. He was lying face up on the carpet with the behemoth's thumbprints forming a welt on his throat. Moose kneeled beside the body, clutching his wounds. His breathing was heavy and irregular and I knew he would expire in a few minutes.

At that precise moment, the door crashed open and Tennant barged in accompanied by a regiment of eager cops—all of them with their pieces drawn. When they saw what had happened and that I was in control of the situation, they put their gats back in their holsters and formed a semi-circle around the gasping Moose Lebowitz.

Moose looked up at us, wincing from the pain. "It's okay now," he said, trying to smile. "I got revenge. Ten years I said I would, ten years I been planning it. Now I got it."

He winced again, then took his trembling hand from his chest and grabbed Armando's shirt at the buttons. With one swift move, he ripped the shirt open, and I could hear a gasp rise from the cops who were standing in the huddle, watching.

"Meet Peaches Moskowitz," Moose said.

Those were his last words.

❑

While the paramedics hauled Quinn into an ambulance and the coroner examined the two dead bodies in the house, I explained the elements of the case to a somewhat baffled Tennant. I told him that the grave at Forest Lawn had been empty, that ten years ago Peaches Moskowitz had faked her death and reappeared as Armando Eclair, hairdresser extraordinaire, that Elvira Swann had been Peaches' twin sister from Milwaukee, that Armando had killed Jack in order to frame Kahn and then had killed Kahn when it began to look like the agent was going to be around long enough to spill the beans. I must have told the whole gruesome tale three times before Tennant finally caught on.

There were a couple of questions still unanswered, but their solutions soon came to light. Though Elvira Swann and Peaches were identical twins, there was one small trait they didn't share—Peaches had a large mole on the inside of her right thigh while the Swann dame did not. It was a small point, but it explained why Moose had killed Elvira Swann, only to discover that she wasn't Peaches. Presumably, Moose had known that Peaches had a twin sister and, after murdering the Swann dame, had hid out near the scene of the crime and followed me, hoping that I would lead him to his victim.

"Oh, by the way," Tennant said, as Moose's body went by on a stretcher, "here's Quinn's lighter back." I took it and put it in my pocket, amazed that Tennant hadn't accidentally shot himself in the foot with it. But then Tennant didn't smoke.

They let Quinn out of the hospital the next day and, since I felt I owed her an apology, I drove over to her place on my way to the airport. I found her looking lucid and alert again, as if her bout with the Neiman paintings had been nothing but a bad dream.

"If I invite you in," she said, "will you promise not to swipe anything this time?"

With my tail between my legs, I nodded and brushed past her into the room. "Okay, okay," I said. "I guess I deserved that. But with a layout like this, can you blame me for suspecting you?"

She shook her head. "All you had to do was ask," she said. "For your information, when Jack was killed I was vacationing in Vegas. I go there about four times a year. You see, I'm quite adept at poker. Championship class. I'm surprised Jack didn't tell you that."

"He didn't."

She shrugged. "Well," she said, "it's all water under the proverbial bridge now, I guess."

I nodded. "One thing I still don't get," I said. "How'd you figure Eclair as the murderer?"

"The combination of a wild hunch and a little bit of luck," Quinn offered. "I wanted to see if I could one-up Tennant on the Lebowitz case so, just for the hell of it, I took out my old school file on Lebowitz. It was pure chance really, but I came upon an old yellowed newspaper clip advertising the charms of Peaches Moskowitz, who'd been a stripper way back then. The face looked awfully familiar, but I couldn't place it at first. Then it hit me—Elvira Swann was really Peaches Moskowitz!"

I scratched my head. "But you were wrong," I said.

"I know, but I was on the right track," she said. "The rest was pure luck. See, one of my bad habits is I can't resist drawing mustaches on pictures. So naturally, while

I was staring at that photo of Peaches, I started doodling on it—and lo and behold, Peaches became Armando!"

"Lady," I said, slapping on my fedora, "you're a helluva dick. I really mean that too. I take my hat off to you and to my old pal Jack, who knew what he was doing when he teamed up with you. So," I added as I headed for the door, "please accept my deepest apologies for ever doubting your prowess. And I'm not the kind of guy who apologizes too often. Especially to dames."

"Thanks," she said, seeing me out, "but aren't you forgetting something?"

"What?"

She sighed heavily. "My lighter."

I couldn't help blushing a little as I dug in my pocket and handed over the revolver-shaped gizmo. She examined it for a second while I pulled a cigarette out of my pack and stuck it in my mouth.

"Allow me," she said, placing the lighter's fake chamber under my unlit butt, the barrel pointed at my Adam's apple. I froze with fright as her finger slowly pressed the trigger.

I was lucky. The bullet only grazed my cheek.